❧·*The Hidden Cove*·❧

**Center Point
Large Print**

**This Large Print Book carries the
Seal of Approval of N.A.V.H.**

ॐ श्री गणेशाय नमः

The ❧· *Hidden* ·❧ *Cove*

A Novel by
Catherine M. Rae

Center Point Publishing
Thorndike, Maine

This Center Point Large Print edition
is published in the year 2000 by arrangement with
St. Martin's Press.

The text of this Large Print edition is unabridged.
In other aspects, this book may vary from the original
edition. Printed in Thailand. Set in 16-point Plantin
type by Bill Coskrey.

ISBN 1-58547-035-X

Library of Congress Cataloging-in-Publication Data

Rae, Catherine M., 1914-
    The hidden cove / Catherine M. Rae.
      p. cm.
    ISBN 1-58547-035-X (lib. bdg. : alk. paper)
    1. Women artists--Fiction. 2. New York (N.Y.)--Fiction. 3. Large type books. I. Title.

PS3568.A355 H53 2000
813'.54--dc21

                                        00-029031

❧·*The Hidden Cove*·❧

For Mary Louise

❧ · *Chapter I* · ❧

WHENEVER JOHN IRELAND took me on board one of the ships riding at anchor in the East River, or tied up at one of the docks that bordered South Street, he kept me close to him while he made his first tour of inspection. That part was all right; I felt safe as long as he held my hand in his large, warm one. But later in the night, if I woke up and found myself alone in the cabin, the creakings and groanings of the ship terrified me. Then I would cry out, and call his name until he came hurrying back from some other part of the ship.

Ever so much better were the nights when we stayed home in the three-room flat Mama had struggled so hard to make comfortable. She was an accomplished seamstress, and even after she took sick she'd sit in the easy chair near the window, sewing fancy trimming on dresses or making lace collars and cuffs for the dressmakers on Broome Street. While she sewed I would sit perched on the stepstool we used to reach the top shelves in the kitchen and make sketches of the church on the corner and the houses across the street, all of which she would declare suitable for framing.

Sometimes, when I could see that she wasn't feeling too cheerful, I would try to amuse her by imitating the way our landlady, Mrs. Diebel, spoke when she was trying to be elegant, or else I would copy Mrs. Copoli's shrill voice when she scolded Aldo or Carmela in the flat above us. Mama would laugh then and say she would never have to worry about me, that I could always make a living as an artist or an actress, whichever I fancied. Either one would probably pay better than sewing, she said.

I never knew how much she was paid for her work, but it must have been enough for her to buy the rugs and furniture that we gradually accumulated, all used articles, of course. She had a good eye for quality, my mother did, and could spot a bargain quicker than most. She once paid a boy ten cents to carry home a small loveseat someone had put out with the trash, and reupholstered it herself. She took her time over it, waiting until she found just the remnants she wanted at the dressmakers' establishments, but that was one occasion when she wasn't satisfied with her work.

"It's perfectly beautiful, isn't it, little love?" she asked as we stood admiring the finished product. Then she laughed and hugged me. "Too bad it isn't more comfortable to sit on! Perhaps I can persuade Mrs. Diebel to take it instead of next month's rent!"

Mrs. Diebel wasn't actually our landlady; she was the housekeeper of the tenement, and she lived in the first floor front, just below our rooms. She kept the halls and stairs remarkably clean, collected the rents once a month for the absent landlord, and reported those tenants she deemed undesirable. In return for her services she was, according to rumor, permitted to live practically, if not entirely, rent free in the most desirable flat in the building. We were all somewhat afraid of her, and although the rules said that the housekeeper was not allowed inside a tenant's flat, Mama and I made a point of keeping our rooms as neat and clean as possible. We'd been told that Mrs. Diebel had a master key and that she was not above snooping when people were out, but that may not have been true. In any case, we made a practice of smiling and wishing her a polite good day whenever we met her in the hall or on the stairs.

"She may be a bit of a dragon, Emmy

darlin'," Mama said one afternoon when we heard the housekeeper berating poor little Mrs. Maloney for allowing her children to come into the vestibule with wet shoes, "but this place is a palace compared to some I've known."

She sat quietly for a few minutes, deftly winding into a ball the yarn I held for her, and I knew she was thinking of the dismal quarters we'd had in various parts of the city after Papa died in an accident down on the docks. I was only five at the time, and there are things I do not remember too clearly, but I know that in spite of Mama's efforts we were soon paupers, evicted from the little house on Ann Street and forced into a series of cheap lodgings, one worse than the one before it. The last one, over on Charlton Street, was by far the meanest, a single room in a filthy tenement, where one dirty sink in an even dirtier hall served four families. It was there that Mama's cough got so bad, and there that John Ireland, Mama's brother, found us.

"Why do we call him John Ireland?" I asked after he'd moved us into Mrs. Diebel's establishment. "Why not just John?"

"Oh, that goes way back," Mama answered with a smile. "You see, darlin', there were so many Johns and Johnnies in the old neighborhood in Dublin where we lived that we took to calling them by their full names—Johnnie O'Brien, John Boyle, John Leary—and somehow John Ireland has stuck all these years. I was never anything but Gracie, though, never Gracie Ireland. And then I married your father and became Grace Adair, and then you came, little Emily Adair.

"To think of it," she continued, shaking out the skirt she'd been hemming, "just think of it: John Ireland, my little brother, the one who was always up to some kind of mischief or other so that no one had any high hopes for him—and he turned out to be—"

"To be the best feller on the block! I heard you maligning me, oh sister mine. Now what am I to make of that?"

Big, ruddy John Ireland stood in the doorway, beaming at us for a moment before putting an assortment of packages on the table and taking off his seaman's coat.

"Ah, it's good to be home and warm," he said, pulling out his pipe and tobacco and sitting down in the squeaky rocking chair Mama had refinished. "And we'll have a real feast tonight! Flounder fresh from the fisherman's net, so fresh it will swim away if you don't eat it fast, Emmy love. And Gracie, I brought some lemon and honey for that cough. Remember how the mother used to make it for us?"

All that was before Mama's cough became bad, really bad, when the three of us were happy together. We weren't rich by any means, but with what Mama earned with her needle and John Ireland's wages from the shipping company we were better off than most of the families in that part of New York in the late 1840s. Sometime during those years I learned that my mother's brother had run away to sea when he was fifteen, worked his way up to being first mate on a cargo ship, and then decided he'd had enough of the stormy waters of the wide Atlantic.

"Nothing like terra firma after all those years of slipping and sliding around the decks in all kinds of weather, I tell you. Lucky I was that Mosher and Company needed someone to supervise the loadings and unloadings, yes sir. And then there's always the extra to be made every so often when they're short of a night watchman. A good life, that it is, yes sir, a good life."

"And mighty lucky for us that you decided to come ashore when you did, John Ireland," Mama said softly.

"Ah, yes, a bit of luck there, Gracie. I minded somehow that it was on Ann Street where you and Teddy Adair lived, and that neighbor of yours—"

"Bella Morrissey," Mama said.

14

"That's the one. There were tears in her eyes when she told me how you'd gone from place to place and ended up in a room on Charlton Street. And what a devil of a time I had findin' which room!"

John Ireland may have seen me shudder at the memory of that place, because he stood up suddenly and said he needed my help in the preparation of the fish feast.

"You chop the onion, Emmy, and add a bit of celery, while I clean this noble swimmer of the deep, and we'll surprise your ma with a dish fit for a queen."

He couldn't do enough for Mama, and as she began to fail more noticeably he redoubled his efforts to ease the pain she strove to hide. He seldom came home empty-handed. I remember mostly the delicacies he brought to tempt her poor appetite: hothouse grapes, Seville oranges, a bottle of Spanish sherry, things like that.

"Try a piece of this soda bread, Gracie," he urged. "Put some of that good butter on it. You know the doctor said we must build you up, and how can we do that if you eat such a little mite?"

She did try, right up to the end, and then one gray morning in December 1850, she simply did not wake up. The dark days right after her death are a blur in my mind except for the crying. I remember that, because I couldn't seem to control it. John Ireland was the most patient of men, but after a while my sobbing must have grated on his nerves.

"Look here, Emmy honey," he said abruptly one evening after telling me to sit down at the kitchen table with him. "Put that handkerchief away and listen to me. I have a plan for us. We don't have to move away from here because your ma is gone; I make enough to keep us. But, you see, I have to be away from you most of the day, and it wouldn't be good for you to stay here alone."

"I wouldn't mind—"

"I know that, honey, but just the same I couldn't rest easy. You should be in school, where you'd be with girls your own age. Now, there's Miss Phoebe Rossiter's classes just over on Henry Street. If you went there that would take care of most of the day. Only thing that worries me is that there'll be times when they'll want me to fill in when one of the watchmen is drunk or sick—"

"I'm not a baby—" I protested.

"Of course you're not. You're a grown-up ten-year-old girl, but I'd be gone all night, honey, not just for a few hours. Ah, well, I'll think of something. Come, put on your coat and bonnet and we'll go over to Gerbacher's

16

and see if we can get some decent meat for an Irish stew. Then we'll see if we can make one as tasty as your grandma did when I was a boy."

⚜

By the end of that week we had things running pretty smoothly. At Miss Phoebe Rossiter's school I found I was ahead in reading (Mama had seen to that), fairly good at my numbers, but woefully bad at penmanship. I could no more balance a penny on my wrist while I wrote than I could fly, nor could I make perfect Ms and Ns the way Loretta Lindstrom did. I can still picture her at the desk next to mine, her blond head bent over her work, her tongue protruding slightly, and the penny steady on her wrist as she slowly and carefully wrote the assigned words.

"I couldn't do it either at first, Emmy," she said one day as we filed down to the basement dining room for our lunch. "And all of a sudden I could. You will, too. You'll see."

There were only twelve of us in the entire school—I'd overheard Miss Phoebe say to John Ireland that not enough parents thought girls were worth educating—and that made it possible for all of us to sit down together in the old-fashioned dining room. Miss Phoebe sat at the head of the table, ladling out the soup or chowder, while her sister, Miss Prudence, sat at the foot and passed the bread and cheese.

"On holidays or birthdays there's cake for dessert," Loretta whispered, "but mostly it's just apples, and sometimes pudding."

"No need to whisper, Loretta," Miss Prudence said with a smile. "Polite conversation is always permissible, you know."

By the end of my first week I think I was in love with Miss Phoebe. Without appearing to try, she commanded our respect and made us anxious to please her; a mere nod of approval from her was enough to produce the same warm glow of satisfaction that I was to feel in later years over a job well done. And she always smelled so nice!

એક

I left the school at four o'clock each day, walked the few blocks to our building, and knocked at Mrs. Diebel's door to let her know that I was home. Sometimes she came upstairs with me to see that I was safely inside our rooms, but if one of her children was crying, or if she was busy with a tenant, I went up alone. I liked that better, because then I wouldn't have to stand and listen politely while she commented on our furnishings.

John Ireland came home shortly after five o'clock and made a big show of being surprised to find the table ready for our supper, set the way Mama had taught me, with the forks on the left, knives and spoons on the right, and napkins next to the forks. Our meals were not elaborate, but they were good, and as time went on he allowed me to do more and more in their preparation—thinking, I am sure, that if I were kept busy I would forget about the empty easy chair near the window.

Things might have gone on that way indefinitely had it not been for the night watchman business. When my uncle came in one cold evening early in February and announced that he had to spend the night on one of Mosher and Company's ships, I tried to convince him that I would be perfectly safe behind our locked door.

"No, lass," he said firmly. "I cannot leave you by yourself. Suppose the house caught fire like the one across the way and you sound asleep in your bed? No, no, it can't be done. And I know no one I'd trust to stay with you. You'll have to come along with me. I'll find a bunk where you can sleep the night through, nice and cozy."

He paused for a moment or two and then sighed. "Damn them," he said softly. "I tried to get out of it, but they would have their way. Ah, well, we'll make the best of it, lass. Come now, we'll have some supper and then be on our way."

·⃕ Chapter II ·⃔

I SAW NOTHING to be afraid of as we approached the waterfront, or on the short trip in the rowboat that took us out to the brig *William Wilson,* and wondered fleetingly why John Ireland kept telling me not to worry, that I'd be safe as houses with him. I was too excited by that time to think of anything but how romantic it was to be rocked to sleep in the cradle of the deep (Emma Willard's song was a favorite with Miss Phoebe). I did, however, give a start when I saw John Ireland transfer a strange-looking object from one pocket of his heavy jacket to another.

"What is that for?" I asked as he helped me up onto the deck.

"Now don't go bothering your head about this," he said quickly, holding up what looked like a metal ball affixed to a handle by a leather strap. " 'Tis only my slungshot, in case I spy a water rat in the hold."

"Would a rat come in here?" I asked anxiously after he'd shown me the neat little cabin in which I was to spend the night.

"Not on your life, honey. Never have I seen one above the waterline, never. Come with me now, and I'll give you the grand tour of the ship, and then we'll settle down here."

Since the *William Wilson* was not a large ship, our grand tour did not last long, only about fifteen minutes, and it wasn't late when we returned to the cabin. Even so, John Ireland made me lie down on a narrow bunk, where he covered me with a patchwork quilt he found in a locker. Then he sat down in what he called a captain's chair—it didn't look nearly as comfortable as the easy chair at home—and lit his pipe. I thought I would lie awake, watching the smoke curling up around his head, so that I would be ready to go with him on his next inspection tour, but either the gentle rocking of the ship or general exhaustion caused me to sleep soundly until he woke me, saying it was well past sunup and the day man had come aboard.

ॐ

"Maybe you'd best not mention this little excursion to anyone, honey," he said as we walked briskly home after being rowed ashore by a sleepy-looking sailor. "It might—"

"Why ever not?" I was astonished. "Miss Phoebe is always asking us to tell about anything interesting we did, and—"

"It's interesting, all right," he agreed, "but I have a feelin' Miss Phoebe might not like it."

"But John Ireland! I was going to tell them all about the inspection and the slungshot—"

"No, honey, please don't. I wouldn't want you put out of the school. You see, river folk are a tough lot, and if Miss Phoebe and Miss Prudence, a prim and proper pair if I ever saw one, thought you were havin' to do with them, why, like as not out you'd go. Mark my words."

I was crestfallen, so ready had I been to boast about my experience, but later on, over breakfast, when I remembered some of the rough characters we'd passed on the docks, I saw his point. I pictured Miss Phoebe and Miss Prudence in their neat silk dresses and my classmates in their ginghams and starched pinafores listening to my description of my night on the river not with delighted interest but with expressions of polite disdain on their faces. They wouldn't have had to put me out; I would have dissolved in tears and fled.

All day long, though, the *William Wilson* was not far from my thoughts, and when John Ireland came home from work he found me at the kitchen table making sketches of the brig and the two rowboats we'd been in.

"I know I can't tell them about it," I said when he had praised my drawings, "but the next time we have an art lesson from Miss Prudence maybe I can draw one of these."

⛬

By the end of May I had spent a total of five nights on the river, only two of them sleepless on account of stormy weather. I would try to keep John Ireland from seeing how frightened I was by pulling the blanket up over my head, and I think that worked. But no matter how hard I tried I could not keep from crying out if I woke up and found myself alone in the cabin.

"Why do I do that?" I asked him one morning as we left the ship after a rough night. "At home if I wake up I just turn over and go back to sleep."

"It's the strangeness, honey," he answered. "On a ship you hear noises you don't hear at home, the creaking of the masts in the wind, a loose bit of cargo sliding around in the hold, things like that. Don't worry about it. I'm always within call, aren't I? Don't I come at once?"

Of course he did, if not at once at least as

soon as he could. I felt ashamed of acting in such a babyish fashion, especially when I really enjoyed what we came to call our "outings" so much. They had simply become part of our lives, and I assumed they'd go on and on.

⁂

On a mild, cloudless night in June we were rowed out to the *Ellen Gray*, and after making a first inspection we sat for a while on the deck looking up at the stars before turning in. John Ireland told me that many a time on a night like that he'd slept on the deck of his ship under the sky rather than with the others in the bunk room.

"There's nothing like it, honey," he said softly, "nothing like it on a calm night in a warm climate."

"Don't you miss it?" I asked.

"*That* I miss, yes, but not the other, not the wind and the rain and the fifty-foot waves. No, all in all I'm better off on land these days."

And he would have been far better off had he been on land that lovely June night.

⁂

Toward morning, just before dawn it must have been, I awoke to find John Ireland standing over me with his slungshot in his hand and an angry look on his face.

"Quiet!" he whispered. "Not a sound!"

With that he pulled the blanket up over my head, and a moment later I heard him leave the cabin. Slight sounds came from the deck, cautious footsteps, as if someone were trying to approach without being heard, and then silence, a dreadful silence. I huddled beneath the blanket, scarcely daring to breathe, and hoping the thudding of my heart would not be heard. Suddenly there were shouts, thumps, cries of pain, and the sound of a heavy body falling.

I heard nothing further until the door of the cabin burst open and rough hands snatched the blanket from me. The two burly young men who stared down at me were as speechless as I was, but not for long. Suddenly the taller of the two began to laugh—not a nice laugh at all— and pinched my cheek. When I began to cry he told me to shut up or he'd pinch me where it really hurt.

"What'll we do with her?" asked the shorter one, moving closer to have a better look at me. "Throw her overboard?"

"Don't be stupider than you hafta, Jimmy," the first one said. "Can't you see what a bit of luck we have here? If we take her to Hasty he'll pay somethin'. Git that chest into the rowboat—no, don't open it, ya dolt. That's where the loot is—then come back here."

"But Nick—"

"Do it!"

"Awright, awright!"

"John Ireland—where—" I began.

"Shut up, you," the one called Nick said, pinching my arm this time.

I began to cry again, and kept on crying while he bundled me in the blanket and carried me out to the deck.

"Put 'er on top of Johnson," I heard the one called Jimmy say, while I struggled to get away from his partner. The blanket fell back from my head, and the last thing I saw before I felt myself falling was the crumpled body of my uncle huddled up against the rail of the ship. A moment later I landed on top of a man lying in the bottom of a rowboat, and after that I remember nothing until I woke up in a small, dark room full of strangers.

⊰ · *Chapter III* · ⊱

I T MAY HAVE been because the light was dim
and the room no larger than the cabin in
which I had spent the night that it seemed
so crowded. Actually there were only six people
there beside myself: four adults and two children. I lay still, thinking that if they thought I
was still asleep they would go away, in which
case I would slip out the door that faced me
and make my way home. Then I remembered
John Ireland's body lying on the deck of the
Ellen Gray, and almost cried out. I must have
made some slight sound, for a woman leaned
over me (she smelled strongly of garlic) and
called out, "She's come to, Jack. What now?"

She straightened up and motioned to a tall
man dressed entirely in black, who for some
reason kept his top hat on in the house.

"Ay," he responded in a deep, almost gut-
tural voice as he came over to look at me. "Ay,

what now? A good question."

He turned suddenly to the two young men standing near the window, looking so angry that I thought he was going to lash out at them. He didn't, though. He stood towering over the youths and spat out a stream of oaths at them in a low, threatening voice that was far more frightening than if he had shouted at them. Listening to him berate them I gathered that they were members of a gang called the Daybreak Boys, whose mission it was to board ships in the river just before dawn, knock out the watchman, and make off with whatever valuables they could lay their hands on.

"And what do you two idiots do?" Jack's voice was ominous. "You let Johnson get blind drunk and leave him in the bottom of the row-boat—God knows where he is now—you kill the watchman when you know you're just supposed to knock him out, then all you bring here is a chest full of rags, and on top of that you bring me a child, a girl at that, not even a lad who might be useful."

"We could teach 'er, Jack," said the one I now recognized as Jimmy.

"You couldn't teach a fish to swim," growled the tall man. "Get outta here, both of you. An' don't come back til you've got somethin' that clinks."

Serves them right, I thought, as I watched my captors slink from the room. Instead of being rewarded for bringing me here all they got was a dressing down. After they left, the room was quiet while Jack and his wife spoke to each other in voices too low for me to distinguish the words. They paid no attention to me when I threw off the blanket, the same one John Ireland had tucked around me the night before, the one I'd been wrapped in when I was thrown into the rowboat.

I sat up, straightened my dress as best I could, and smoothed my hair back from my face. The ribbons I'd tied on my braids were gone, and tears sprang into my eyes when I remembered how John Ireland would marvel at the neat bows I could make. Don't cry, I said to myself, don't think about John Ireland. Maybe he's all right, maybe he just fell. Think about how to get out of here.

"Excuse me," I said in a loud voice, "but I'm hungry. Could I—"

"Shut yer mouth," Jack growled.

"Git 'er some bread and cheese," the woman said to a girl about seven or eight. "Listen to me, Jack. If you want to use 'er, you can't have her faintin' away."

"I'd like to go home, please," I said, suddenly terrified at the thought of being "used"

31

by this man—whatever that meant.

I found out soon enough. They watched me eat the stale bread and the piece of hard cheese the girl brought in, and when the cracked (and none too clean) plate was empty Jack stared at me for a few moments before turning to his wife.

"She's real pretty, Mag," he said. "Look at that face! Maybe I'll keep her. Take 'er upstairs. Can't have 'er runnin' off on us."

"No!" I cried. "Let me go! I want to go home and—"

"Now you look 'ere, Jack Hasty," Mag shouted. "Pretty girls is all right to make money on, but not to have in my house. You can't—"

"I can do as I like," he snapped, "an' it ain't your house! If I take a fancy—"

"I know your fancies," she cried. "She's not stayin'."

"I say she is!" he retorted, "an' what I say goes. Lookit that face, tears an' all—she's a beauty, an' I'm keepin' 'er! Now take 'er upstairs, hear?"

"Please, please let me go!" I begged. "Please—"

It was no use. When Jack Hasty took out a cigar and busied himself lighting it, the woman grabbed me by the hair, forced me up a narrow flight of stairs, and pushed me so roughly into a small room half filled with crates and boxes that I stumbled and banged my arm on one of them. I was too dazed to feel any pain. I simply sank down on the nearest crate and listened to Mag's retreating footsteps.

I don't know how long I stayed in there, staring at the single dirty window the room afforded, but after a while I was conscious of voices coming from below. The kitchen must have been directly underneath the room I was in; I could hear the clatter of pots and dishes and smell bacon frying. Apparently the family had gathered for their evening meal.

I didn't dare move any of the boxes around for fear they'd hear me, but by stepping carefully over some of the smaller ones and keeping my eyes on the floor I discovered a knothole in a board through which the sounds came relatively clearly. I won't attempt to repeat everything I heard, for I cannot remember all of it. Suffice it to say that I found out who the Hastys were, what they did, and more important, what they had in mind for me.

I gathered that they were thieves, and when I heard Jack Hasty ask Mag if all the boxes and crates were tied up securely I was convinced that I was surrounded by stolen goods. What would they do with it all? I wondered. Sell it? And to whom? Did it all come from ships anchored in the East River, or did they also rob the houses of rich people? I didn't know it then, but several years were to elapse before I was to know the answers to these questions.

As I listened I realized that Hasty was the leader of a group of river pirates known as the Daybreak Boys, so called because they robbed ships just at dawn, before the harbor police were about. Then the conversation shifted to me: Had I been a boy they would have forced me to become a member of the gang, but since I was a girl I was to be taken to someone known as Fat Sally, who could certainly "use" me. Mag had evidently won that argument with Hasty. When I heard him say that one more watchman was gone and that no one would ever find out who did it, I knew for certain that John Ireland was dead, and once again tears streamed down my face.

After a while I curled up on the floor against one of the boxes and stared at the dusty window, watching the daylight fade and wondering how I could evade the Hastys and the woman known as Fat Sally. I had a feeling it would not be easy to do.

❧·*Chapter IV*·❧

J<small>ACK SAYS YOU</small> kin 'ave this 'un fer two dollars, Sal," Mag said to the enormous woman who stood in the doorway of a shop on Hester Street. "She's small enough fer you, and spry, quick as a flash."

"Lemme lookit 'er," the fat woman said, pulling me into the shop, which smelled like John Ireland's pipe tobacco. She was dressed in a low-necked, loose-fitting garment that hung from her shoulders and almost reached the floor. Brilliants of some sort encircled her short, thick neck, and on both hands she wore three or four rings. I was trying to count them when she suddenly unbuttoned my dress and whipped it over my head, leaving me standing in my camisole and underpants. I looked at Mag for help, but she never took her eyes off Fat Sally.

"The dress itself is wuth two dollars, Sal," she said, holding out her hand. I knew the

35

dress had cost four dollars, but I was too stunned to say anything as I watched Sal hand some bills to Mag, who grabbed them and left the place without another word. I think I would have chosen her over Fat Sal, who now had a grip on my arm; at least she didn't take my dress away from me.

"Inside with you, missy," Sally said, folding my dress over her arm. "Too late to learn you anything tonight. Tomorrer we'll begin. Dancer will take you in hand, and next day ye'll start to earn yer keep."

ৠ

From the beginning, life at Fat Sally's establishment was worse than anything I had ever dreamed of, far worse than living in poverty with Mama had been. That first night I was shown into a room over the shop where five other girls were lying on the floor with only dirty rags to cover them. Sally handed me what looked like part of an old tablecloth and told me to find a place to lie down. I'd need my sleep for tomorrow, she said, and disappeared, locking the door behind her.

A pale, dirty, thin-faced girl sat up and motioned me to a place next to her, and from her I learned where I was and what was expected of me. Her name, she said, was Piggy, because on her first day all she could steal was a pig's foot from the butcher.

"But why," I asked, genuinely puzzled. "Why did you steal a pig's foot?"

"All I could get," she answered. "Else I'd 'ave come back with nothin'. An' did I ever git a beatin'!"

"I still don't understand."

"She makes us steal, see? An' if ya don't bring back money or somethin' she likes she gits mad. Boy, kin she git mad!"

"Why do you come back here, then?" I asked. "Why don't you run away?"

"An' where'd I go?" she responded. "Back to sleepin' in doorways? This ain't no hotel, but it's better'n the street. Anyways, she'd have Dancer or Gussie find me, an' then there'd be hell to pay."

"Who are they, Dancer and Gussie?"

"Her kids. An' they're worsen she is. She's bad enough when she's mad, but Dancer—ow— you don't wanna have him after ya, and Gussie, she'd like to pull yer hair out by the roots. So don't try runnin' away. Now go to sleep."

With that she pulled part of a curtain around her and turned over. I spread the piece of tablecloth over me as best I could, and despite the hard floor and the lack of a pillow for my head, I slept. I was dreaming of being in a rowboat with John Ireland, listening to the sound of a bell buoy come across the water, when Piggy poked me in the back.

"Git up! Git up!" she whispered hoarsely. "She's here awready—Gussie!"

I sat up slowly, stiff all over. A tall young woman in a white silk dress stood in the doorway of our mean little room, beating two pot covers together and shouting at us to "git a move on." When I hung back as the others headed for the stairs, Gussie took me by the arm and pushed me ahead of her. When I protested that I was still in my underwear, she struck me across the back with one of the pot covers, causing me to stumble and almost fall down the steep flight of stairs.

"The terlct's over there," she said, pointing to an outhouse behind the building. "Git goin'!"

Most of what happened that day is a merciful blur in my mind, but some things will always stand out clearly. After we'd taken turns using the filthy, primitive facilities in the outhouse we were herded into a large kitchen and told to hurry up and eat the watery gruel that was already set out on the table. After one mouthful I put my spoon down and stared miserably across at Piggy. She was gobbling up the unsavory mess as if it were the best food

38

she'd ever tasted, and when she caught my eye she made motions with her spoon that I interpreted as signals that I should follow her example. I couldn't.

Suddenly all five girls disappeared, and I found myself being taken by the impatient Gussie to a completely different part of the house. At the end of a dim passageway she knocked on a heavy wooden door before throwing it open to expose a spacious room that looked to me like a parlor fit for a queen. Fat Sally sat enthroned in a large armchair next to a marble fireplace, with a substantial breakfast set on a table in front of her. The room was furnished with thick rugs of various designs, sofas and chairs covered in velvets and silks, and several large cupboards, chests, tables, and the like. I had time to take all this in while the mistress of the house finished eating. When I took a step toward the mantel to get a better look at the painting that hung over it, Gussie took hold of one of my braids and yanked me back.

Fat Sally put her knife and fork down and stared at me while she wiped her mouth with the back of her hand.

"Git 'er a dress, Gus," she said after studying my features for a moment or two. "That girl Netta was about her size. I put her clothes in one of the bags in the attic."

Gussie left without a word, and for a few moments Fat Sally and I eyed each other.

"You've a bold look to you, missy," she said finally. "But listen to me. You do what yer told and nothin'll happen to you. Don't do what yer told and plenty will happen to you. You've been to school, have you?"

I nodded, and she went on. "Well, this here is a school, a school for pickpockets. When Gussie comes back with somethin' fer you to wear, then Dancer'll give you some pointers. And tomorrer you start to work. See?"

I nodded again, thinking that even if a hundred Gussies and Dancers came after me, as soon as I was outside I'd run away, back to our rooms and Mrs. Diebel. Fat Sally could have been reading my mind.

"I knows what yer thinkin', missy," she said, shaking one of her beringed fingers at me, "an' I'm warnin' you not to try anything. I knows how to break the stubborn ones. Ah, here's Gus. Put that dress on now and lemme see."

The plain gray dress Gussie handed me had a three-cornered tear in one sleeve, as if the wearer had caught it on a nail, and a series of stains down the front. I thought they were from some kind of black grease, but that night Liz, a skinny, sharp-faced girl with crossed eyes, pointed a dirty finger at me and giggled.

"Blood," she said, hopping from one foot to the other. "That's Netta's blood from where the fella twisted her arm and made her cut herself with her own knife."

That was later, though. For the rest of my first day at Fat Sally's, her son, Dancer, a mean-looking youth of fifteen or sixteen, started me on the fundamentals of picking pockets. First he took my hand in his and demonstrated the different ways of slipping it into a man's pocket or a lady's bag.

"An' if she's carryin' a reticule, one of them string bags on 'er wrist, ya takes yer knife an' quick as a flash ya cuts it off like this. See?"

He handed me a sharp-edged instrument that looked more like a dagger than a knife and made me practice cutting lengths of string that he wound around an old spoon and let dangle carelessly from his wrist. When I'd done that to his satisfaction he offered more advice.

"An' if ya see a gent, a likely lookin' one, an' ya want 'is purse, what ya do is start yellin' 'Look Out!' an' pointin' across the street or somewheres, and when 'e looks ya snatch the purse outta 'is pocket. Then ya scarper, scarper real fast."

Sometime during that endless day—it must have been well past noon—I felt weak and told Dancer I was hungry.

"Hungry, are ya? Come on, then. I'll learn ya how to git some vittles."

Before I realized what he meant we were out of the house, around the corner, and through a garbage-strewn alley, at the end of which we came to a narrow street where peddlers of fish, meat pies, and sorry-looking baskets of fruit were crying their wares. I don't know how Dancer did it, but without letting go of my wrist, which he'd been holding the entire time, he managed to steal one of the pies, a half-rotten orange, and a perfect banana.

"Think ya could do it?" he asked when we were sitting in the shade of a stone wall next to a churchyard, well away from the street of peddlers. I nodded, chewing away at the meat pie, which he had divided in half.

"Yer awright, Em," he went on, "but ya gotta talk different. Try to talk like me."

"Awright," I said, trying not to laugh. "I kin talk like ya if I wanna."

"Crikey, that's good! Yer awright!" He looked at me in surprise. "See, no need ta ever go hungry, ya just gotta know how ta do it. Here, ya want some of this banana? It's a good 'un."

He nodded complacently and leaned back against the wall. Maybe I can get away now, I thought, watching him half close his eyes, but when I looked away, wondering in which direction to run, he took hold of my wrist again and said it was time to go.

৺

"She'll do good, Ma," he said when we entered the kitchen and found Fat Sally watching the cook (a woman almost as large as herself) pluck a chicken. "She's small an' quick. An' she kin run. I tried 'er out. An' I'm learnin' 'er to talk like me."

"Tomorrer," Sally said, eyeing me sternly. "Tomorrer we'll see what she kin do."

৺

"Why is he called Dancer?" I asked Piggy that night after the six of us had devoured the chicken and were locked in our dismal room. "What kind of name is that?"

"Who knows?" she answered wearily. "Mebbe because he danced away from the coppers so many times. Mebbe he likes the name."

She pulled her piece of curtain around her and closed her eyes. A moment later she opened them again and said she thought Netta's dress looked better on me than it had on her.

"What happened to Netta?" I asked. "Where did she go?"

"Oh, she died, blood poison or somethin'," Piggy said with a yawn. "Now fer the luva Pete, go to sleep."

⪫· *Chapter V* ·⪪

THE NEXT DAY was a disaster. I stood for a moment in front of the shop, watching Piggy and the other girls run off in different directions, and wondered how far I would get on my way back to Mrs. Diebel's before Gussie or Dancer caught up with me.

"Tomorrer Dancer'll git you a knife," Fat Sally had said when I stood up from the breakfast table leaving my bowl of gruel untouched. "Today use yer fingers, and don't try anythin' 'less you want to go cryin' to bed, hear?"

One of the girls, Lally Ally they called her, who had brought in a lady's bag and a silk handkerchief the day before, told me to try Broadway, and after a while I began to walk in the direction I had seen her take. Walk! That's all I did the whole day long, up one street and down another, without even half a meat pie to sustain me. From time to time I'd look behind me, and once I thought I saw Dancer following me, but I couldn't be sure.

Sometime after noon I was resting on a doorstep when a fire wagon went by, and a boy who was running alongside it dropped something. He didn't miss it, and after he went on I picked up a little cloth bag of marbles. He must have had a hole in his pocket.

I was walking aimlessly along, swinging the bag of marbles from my wrist and thinking that at least I had something to show Fat Sally, when suddenly I lost it. The small boy I saw darting in and out of the crowd ahead of me had used his knife exactly the way Dancer had showed me and left me with nothing but a piece of string dangling from my arm. I ran after him but had to give up when I came to the corner of Oliver Street and could no longer see him. I continued on toward the East River, occasionally glancing behind me to see if I were being followed, without an idea in my head about how to escape a beating for returning empty-handed.

Maybe I'll find a slungshot down here, I said to myself, and instead of giving it to Fat Sally I'll whack her with it. The thought cheered me, but not as much as the sight that greeted my eyes when I arrived at the docks. A cart laden with bags of sugar had overturned, and a crowd of ragged women and children were scooping up what they could in pails and even in their hats, while the carter tried to chase them off. I watched them for a moment or two before spying an open bag lying under the cart itself. I slipped behind one of the wheels, snatched it away from a boy who had crawled beneath the cart from the other side, and made off with it, unnoticed in the melee.

Fat Sally boxed my ears, saying it wasn't worth much since it was only half full and if I didn't do better I'd get a real beating.

"Purses, money, rings," she shouted. "Git some of them!"

૭ઠ

When I started out the next day I had no intention of stealing any money or jewelry or anything else. I was determined to go to Mrs. Diebel and throw myself on her mercy. I'd offer to take care of her children or scrub the hall, or sweep the steps—whatever she wanted me to do if only she'd let me stay.

Gussie and Dancer were nowhere to be seen as I rounded the corner, still wearing the dirty gray dress and fingering the handle of the knife that was in my pocket—or rather, holding on to it so that the sharp blade didn't cut into my thigh. I reached the tenement on Water Street without incident and stood for a moment, looking up at the window where Mama had so often sat, before I lifted the heavy brass knocker.

I heard Mrs. Diebel's heavy tread, and as the door swung open I smiled in anticipation of her welcome, only to be struck dumb when she shouted that she wanted no beggars or ragamuffins on her doorstep. With that she slammed the door, and when I heard her put the chain across I began to cry.

"Please, Mrs. Diebel, please," I sobbed. "It's Emily, Emily Adair! Please let me in!" There was no response. "I know I'm all dirty," I cried, "but I just need to get cleaned up and find my own clothes. Please!"

Years later I heard from Carmela Capoli, who had lived on the floor above us, that the housekeeper had helped herself to whatever she wanted from our rooms before letting them to an elderly couple.

૱

After a while I wandered slowly down to the docks again, following the route John Ireland and I had taken. I had no particular plan in mind as I made my way through the bustling activity of South Street, glancing from time to time at the tall ships at their moorings, but I knew that if I didn't find a place to sleep that night I'd have to go back, even empty-handed, to Fat Sally's. As Piggy had said, it was better than sleeping in the street.

I paused for a moment to watch heavy bales of cotton being loaded onto a ship bearing the name *Seabird*, and when I turned to go on I was startled to see Jimmy and Nick, the two Daybreak Boys who had murdered John Ireland, standing nearby. My heart almost stopped when one of them looked straight at me, but he gave no sign of recognition. Two and a half days at Fat Sally's had made a different person of me, externally at least.

I slipped away into the crowd, paying little attention to where I was going—I was just anxious to put some distance between me and those two ruffians—when I turned my ankle on the uneven pavement. I stumbled against a passerby and caught hold of his coattails to keep from falling on the unforgiving cobblestones. I heard my knife fall from my pocket and was looking for it when he spoke.

"Now, now, you're not after my purse, are you, my girl?" asked a deep voice with a hint of a laugh behind it as a strong hand grasped my arm.

"Oh, no sir, no sir. I tripped—my ankle—please let me go, sir!" And I began to cry.

"Hey! Just a minute, let me have a look at you. Don't cry, I won't hurt you." His voice was gentle, and I didn't pull away when he put his hand under my chin so that I had to look up at him. I saw a pleasant face, a handsome one partially shaded by the brim of his hat, a face I liked immediately, and as I stared, a puzzled, startled expression came into his dark brown eyes.

"Please, sir—" I said.

"By God," he murmured, still studying my face carefully. "You look like—what is your name?"

"Emily, sir, Emily Adair."

"Emily Adair, eh? What are you doing here, Emily Adair?"

"I have no place to go, sir. I need a place to sleep tonight. Mrs. Diebel won't let me in to get my clothes, and if I go back to Fat Sally's she'll beat me for not bringing any money. I don't want to go back there, anyway, and I don't know what to do."

"How old are you, Emily?" he asked, still not relinquishing his hold on my arm.

"Ten, sir. Ten last March tenth."

"And your parents? Where are they?"

"They died, sir, and John Ireland, that's my uncle, he was killed by some robbers called the Daybreak Boys."

"So you have no one, eh, Emily?"

"No one, sir, no one at all, and I need—"

"You need a place to sleep tonight, I know. I would like you to come home with me, Emily, and meet my wife. We had a little girl once. She'd be ten now. . . . Will you come with me? You can trust me to do you no harm, and possibly you can do us some good. My name's John Lawrence. What do you say?"

I did trust him, and as I sat beside him in the cab on the way north to Lafayette Street, I felt safe for the first time since I awoke on board the *Ellen Gray*. I also felt incredibly grubby and dirty next to this handsome man, impeccably dressed in a light summer coat with a starched white cravat beneath a soft gray waistcoat.

I started to explain why I was wearing a bloodstained dress, but he stopped me, saying that he would like to hear about that later on, when we weren't rattling over the cobblestones. After a while we drew up in front of a row of houses that I later learned was known as Colonnade Row because of the marble columns that fronted each one.

The door to Number 21 was opened by a cheerful-looking maid wearing a frilly white apron over a blue and white chambray uniform. I knew it was chambray, because once Mama had made me a dress of that very material from remnants one of the dressmakers had given her.

"Tell Nellie to come here, will you, Maria?" Mr. Lawrence said when the girl gasped at the sight of me. "Right away, Maria, please."

The maid darted off, and in a few minutes a pleasant-looking woman dressed in black silk appeared in the archway of the marble entrance hall.

"This is Emily Adair, Nellie," Mr. Lawrence said, putting his hand lightly on my shoulder. "She looks like Ellie, doesn't she?"

"The mirror image of her, sir. Gave me quite a start, she did," the woman replied.

"Take her upstairs, then, clean her up, find some of Ellie's clothes for her—oh, yes, and give her something to eat. Then bring her down to me in the library. And Nellie, on no account go near Mrs. Lawrence."

Nellie looked puzzled, but she nodded to the master of the house and took my hand. She led me up a wide, carpeted staircase and ushered me into what I thought must be the most beautiful, spacious, white and gold bathroom in the world.

જી

Two hours later, scrubbed, brushed, fed, and wearing lacy undergarments beneath a dimity dress with little lavender flowers on it, I was taken down to the library. Mr. Lawrence rose from a chair near the window to greet me and thank Nellie for what he called her "transformation" of me. Then he asked her to tell the cook that a young lady would be dining with him at seven o'clock. I wondered why Mrs. Lawrence would not be there, but he made that clear almost immediately.

"My wife is ill, Emily," he said after inviting me to sit down in front of a window overlooking a garden where flower beds and climbing roses bloomed in the late afternoon sun. "She has not left her room since Ellie's death almost a year ago."

"How did Ellie die, Mr. Lawrence?" I asked.

"Horribly," he answered, looking away from me. "She was trampled to death by a runaway horse. Flora, my wife, had taken her to the milliner's, and because Ellie was recovering from a cold she left the child to sit outside in the sun while she went in to see about her hats. The accident affected my wife's mind; she insists that Ellie will come home again, and in the meantime she cries, night and day, and scarcely touches her food. It breaks my heart to see her, and the doctors—I've had dozens of them in to examine her—can do nothing."

"And you think I—" I began.

"Exactly," he interrupted. "The resemblance is amazing, the deep blue eyes—her mother's eyes—the chestnut hair, the shape of the face—you could be Ellie, and you may be able to make Flora well again. It's a strange thing to ask of a ten-year-old girl, but it means so much to me, Emily. I love my wife dearly and would do anything to see her restored to health. I think, I hope, the mere sight of you will help."

"But do I sound like Ellie when I speak?" I asked doubtfully. "Couldn't Mrs. Lawrence tell?"

"No, you have the same low voice Ellie had—or near enough so that it wouldn't be noticeable. But now, Emily, I want to know all about you. What was your upbringing? It's obvious from your speech and mannerisms that you are not a street urchin. What on earth were you doing in those rags?"

He heard me out without interruption until I mentioned Jack Hasty and how I'd been locked in a room in his house.

"You say there were crates and boxes in that room?" he asked, frowning slightly. "Have you any idea what was in them? No? Ah, well, go on, my dear."

When I told him how surprised I was to see the grand furnishings in Fat Sally's private quarters, he shook his head.

"It's the way of the world, Emily, or rather

the way of the world of crooks and thieves. The ones in control live in luxury at the expense of their hirelings. Fat Sally not only has her pickpockets to steal for her, she also has professional burgulars who unload goods on her and get a percentage of what she sells them for. And of course she keeps whatever she likes for herself. This kind of thing has been going on for centuries and will probably continue until the last day.

"But you don't need to worry about Fat Sally or Gussie or Dancer any longer. You'll be well taken care of here. Ah, I see Maria has come in to announce dinner."

I had never seen a table set like the one in the Lawrence household, with its tall silver candlesticks and bowl of pale pink roses on a snowy white damask tablecloth. The silver gleamed, the crystal sparkled, and the gold border on the delicate china glowed in the soft light. As we ate the perfectly cooked dishes the maid brought in, I wondered if Mrs. Lawrence were as lovely as the furnishings she had chosen for her home.

꒰· Chapter VI ·꒱

LTHOUGH I HEARD the mistress of that magnificent house in Colonnade Row crying softly in her bedroom from time to time, I did not see her immediately. I wasn't quite ready, according to Mr. Lawrence. He, along with Nellie and Madame Fortier, who had been Ellie's governess and was recalled to be mine, spent hours each day coaching me in my impersonation of the dead girl. Even the household staff—the cook and parlor, chamber, and kitchen maids—were called upon to point out Ellie's likes and dislikes. Among other things I learned from Cook that Ellie was forever pestering her to make jam tarts and gingerbread, and the parlormaid told me that the child would race to answer the doorbell whenever it rang. The chambermaid said she was always picking up the clothes Miss Ellie left strewn about in her bedroom, and Anna, the kitchen maid, giggled as she described Ellie's imitation of Cook scolding the iceman for bringing in mud on his boots. I listened to all of them, trying to remember what they said but privately wondering whether any of it would do any good.

Of them all, Nellie was the one who helped me the most. She had, she told me, been with Mrs. Lawrence before her marriage to Mr. Lawrence and came to Colonnade Row with her. Then, when Ellie was born, she acted as nanny to the child, and later when Madame came she was made housekeeper.

"So you see, there isn't much I don't know about Ellie—or the entire household for that matter," she said one afternoon when I was in her little sitting room watching her sew a fresh white collar on one of Ellie's dresses.

"The staff wasn't always the way it is today," she said musingly. "We just had a cook, and not a very good one, and a woman to do the cleaning. The master wasn't happy about the way things were going, and Mrs. Lawrence, poor thing, was no hand at running a house even before she got sick. Many a time I'd find her crying over a burnt meal or a piece of broken wedding china.

"I'd not much to do for Ellie once Madame came, and little by little I began to set things straight. The master noticed—he doesn't miss a trick—and one day he called me into the library and asked me to take full charge. 'I want a well-run household, Nellie,' he said. 'Tell me what is needed and I'll see that you have it.' I told him we should have a better cook, more maids, and so on, and he agreed. 'See to it, then,' he said, 'and don't worry about the expense. And see that my wife is not bothered. I can't have her crying over broken dishes.'

"So," Nellie continued, snipping off a thread and then leaning back in her rocker, "I found a cook first, and then the rest of the maids. I spent some time training them, and everything went along as smoothly as silk until Ellie was killed."

"You loved her, didn't you, Nellie?" I asked after a few moments of silence.

"As if she were my own bairn," she answered, "and it breaks my heart to see the master grieving over what her death has done to Mrs. Lawrence."

"Do you think—" I began and then stopped for fear of sounding bold.

"That she'll take you for Ellie?" she asked, looking over at me. "Who can say? 'Tis a strange malady she has, a sickness of the mind, but perhaps if you remember all we've told you about Ellie—goodness knows, you look enough like her to be her twin sister."

Nurse Hollis, who was in constant attendance upon Mrs. Lawrence, did not, I could tell, think much of the charade we were rehearsing. She was pleasant enough whenever I saw her, but I heard her say to Mr. Lawrence that there might be trouble eventually.

"How will you explain it, sir," she asked, "if Mrs. Lawrence regains all her wits? After all, she saw Ellie's accident, saw her lying dead—how will you explain that she came back to life?"

"We would have to say that Ellie made a miraculous recovery after a long time," he answered.

"Your wife is very ill, Mr. Lawrence, but she is not a stupid woman." Nurse Hollis shook her head.

"I know that, Nurse Hollis. I know there is a chance that this won't work, but I feel there is an equal chance that it will. We shall just have to wait and see."

The other members of the staff seemed to accept me, if not exactly in Ellie's place, at least as a member of the household. Possibly because she was closest to me in age, I liked Anna, the giggly kitchen maid, the best. Sometimes when she was free I sat with her in a corner of the kitchen and watched her work-roughened fingers as she knitted a complicated pattern into a pair of mittens.

"An Irish design, miss," she said one day. "My granny learned me. 'Tis easy, once you get the thumb out of the way. See the blue here, and the red next—I could learn you if you was to bring me some yarn."

And she did "learn" me, after a fashion, but that was later, much later. . . .

⁂

The first time I saw the invalid was on a Sunday morning in July. Mr. Lawrence asked me to wear a hat and gloves, and to carry a prayer book, which surprised me.

"I'll go in with you, Emily," he said, "and we won't stay long. I just want to see if she recognizes Ellie in you. You must say we are on our way to church—that will please her—and then tell her that you'll stop in to see her afterward."

I did exactly as I had been told, but the sick woman paid no attention to me when I said my little piece. She must have been truly lovely, I thought, gazing down at the delicate features and the still glossy dark hair that curled away from her high, alabaster forehead. One slender hand lay motionless on the silken coverlet, while in the other she held a lace-edged handkerchief that she shook out from time to time, releasing the light scent of dried lavender. She said nothing, and she didn't even look at me, not once, but stared fixedly at the foot of the great canopied bed in which she lay, and after a while Mr. Lawrence took my arm and led me from the room. Nurse Hollis followed us into the passageway and said that her patient had had a bad night and was probably exhausted.

"When that happens she simply refuses to speak or respond in any way," she added. "Maybe later today . . ."

⁂

"I do think it is going to work, Emily," Mr. Lawrence said that afternoon as we sat in the garden waiting for tea to be brought out. "When I went in to see her after lunch she was more alert and told me that Ellie had come to see her."

"So she did know I'd been there!" I exclaimed. "And she really thought I was Ellie?"

"Yes, you passed the first test, and I think— I hope—that augurs well. I shall be forever in your debt, Emily Adair, if my Flora recovers. You are happy here, are you not?"

"Oh, yes, Mr. Lawrence."

"Not Mr. Lawrence, my dear. Ellie called me Papa, and if it isn't too much to ask I would like you to do the same. We did talk about how you must call Flora Mama, did we not? Yes, of course we did. If you said Mr. Lawrence in front of her the game would be up, you know."

I nodded but made no direct reply. I had a strange feeling that afternoon that in spite of the comfortable, even luxurious, circumstances in which I found myself, my future was as uncertain as it had been ever since John Ireland was killed. Would I be kept on here if Flora Lawrence recovered, to pass for Ellie Lawrence for the rest of my life? Or, if she saw through the ruse, would I be sent away, turned out into the streets again? Or what if she died? I certainly would not be needed then.

Mr. Lawrence may have had some inkling of what was going through my mind, because after Maria had put down the tea tray and gone back into the house he turned to me and spoke in a low voice.

"No matter what happens, Emily," he said reassuringly, "you are not to worry. I have asked you to perform a difficult, maybe impossible, task, and I feel responsible for you. I am indebted to you. Now, tell me how you are getting on with Madame Fortier. Ellie was quite fond of her, you know."

⛫

On my next two visits to the sickroom, Mrs.

Lawrence merely looked at me for a few moments before closing her eyes, but the third time I went she smiled at me and said in a voice just above a whisper, "Ellie, my darling, I told Papa you would come back."

"Yes, Mama, I am here," I answered, taking her thin hand in mine. "Would you like me to sit with you for a while?"

She nodded, and I stayed until Nurse Hollis came and said Madame was waiting for me. I guessed she thought there was less chance of my giving away my true identity if I didn't stay too long.

Mr. Lawrence was delighted when he heard how successful my visit had been, and Dr. Ramsay, who called three or four times a week, said his patient seemed to be showing signs of improvement. He smiled and nodded, but I thought he emphasized the word "seemed." Nobody else appeared to notice that, though, so I said nothing to Mr. Lawrence.

۞

My days settled down to a pleasant, regular pattern. Mornings were devoted to lessons with Madame, who taught me a great deal about the history of "la belle France," as well as the language of that country. I was grateful that she did not stress penmanship and was happy to solve the simple arithmetic problems she set me. In the afternoons we generally went out "to take the air" for an hour or so, and then I was free to amuse myself with my sketching or a book from Mr. Lawrence's library until it was time for dinner.

And what dinners we had! I had never imagined that such delicious food existed, things like soufflés, salmon poached in wine, delicately seasoned soups, and a variety of tarts and puddings. I always had breakfast and lunch with Madame in the cheerful breakfast room next to the kitchen (and dinner, too, if Mr. Lawrence was out of town visiting his brother, as he often was), but most evenings I took dinner with Mr. Lawrence in the formal oval dining room. I loved the hour after our evening meal, which he and I would spend in his library. Sometimes we merely talked or read, but if he wasn't too tired he'd give me a lesson on chess.

One night when I admired a lacquered box on his desk he smiled and said that it was one of his imports.

"That's what I do for a living, Emily," he explained. "I import beautiful things from all over the world and then sell most of them to those who can afford to buy them."

"Oh, that's why you were down at the docks," I said.

"The day I found you? Yes, I was checking on a shipment of china from England that had been delayed. My office is right near there on John Street, where most of my work is done, but some of it must be done here. That's why I have night visitors, you see, men who are tied up during the day."

And he did indeed have "night visitors," of which we were all aware, although I'd never seen them. At nine o'clock Madame would come into the library for me, never a minute later, for, as she said, Mr. Lawrence must be free to receive those business acquaintances who chose to call in the evening.

Whoever these acquaintances were—and I thought it strange that they should come so regularly—they must have been important, for Mr. Lawrence admitted them himself after the staff had retired and escorted them into the library at the rear of the house. Sometimes I would hear the front door close when they left, but generally I was asleep by that time. I wonder now why I wasn't more curious about them.

※

For the rest of that summer and well into the

fall I visited Mrs. Lawrence twice a day, generally staying for only ten or fifteen minutes, but if she frowned when I stood up to leave, as happened on a few occasions, I would stay longer. Sometimes she would be reclining on a chaise near the window, wearing an elaborately embroidered peignoir, but on most days I found her in bed, propped up on her pillows. She enjoyed hearing about my lessons with Madame Fortier and often asked me where we'd gone for our walk that day, but on the whole she spoke very little, and as far as I could see she had not changed in her appearance since I first saw her.

She had stopped crying, though, Nurse Hollis said, and was sleeping better at night, which made me think that I might be doing some good. Then something happened that made me wonder. One morning I told her that Papa was going to take me to see the exhibits at Barnum's Museum, and her expression suddenly changed. She'd been lying contentedly against her pillows, completely relaxed, when all at once she sat bolt upright and stared hard at me, as if trying to penetrate my skull with her bright blue eyes. After a moment or two she lay back and said that I had better go. The incident puzzled me, but when I mentioned it to Mr. Lawrence he made light of it, saying that she might have associated Barnum's with circus horses and that reminded her of Ellie's accident.

"Just don't mention it again, Emily," he said, and I never did.

❧

The next day Mrs. Lawrence was especially cheerful, welcoming me with a little smile, saying how nice I looked in the gingham dress I was wearing and asking if any roses still were blooming in the garden. We were back on an even keel, and there's no telling how long this might have lasted if *I*, Emily, in spite of all my careful monitoring of my speech and behavior, hadn't made a fatal slip.

On a cool day in mid-October Mr. Lawrence noticed that the coat I had put on was a bit short for me and asked Madame to have me measured for a new one.

"And while you're about it," he said with a smile, "three or four new dresses would not be amiss. Ellie was always after us to get her something new to wear, and you are growing taller, my dear."

Madame and I together chose the materials, a warm brown wool for the coat and bonnet, both of which were to be trimmed with beaver fur, and enough cottons and silks for four dresses. Then, just as we were about to leave the drygoods store, I saw a bolt of glistening crimson velvet, the exact shade of a dress Mama had made for me a few years ago. She'd also made the lace for the collar and cuffs.

"You like that?" Madame asked as I ran my fingers over the soft nap. "Why not have it, then, instead of the green stripe? I think it would suit your coloring better."

In due course my new wardrobe was completed. The coat came home from the tailor, the bonnet from the milliner, and Miss Blanche, the seamstress who came to the house, finished the dresses.

"We will save this one for colder weather," Madame said as she hung the red velvet in my closet. "It is still too mild for it."

I was anxious to wear the dress, but I knew she was right. Mama would have said exactly the same thing.

"But couldn't I try it on to show it to Mrs. Lawrence?" I asked. "She might like to see how it fits."

"Yes," Madame agreed. "She would, of that I am sure. So, someday when it rains and we do not go out we will try it on. It is certain to give her pleasure. *Oui, ma petite, c'est une bonne idée.*" As things turned out it was not at all *"une bonne idée."* Flora Lawrence's eyes were closed as I approached her bed that gloomy day in early

November. I stood quietly, waiting to see if she was really asleep or merely resting. When she gave no sign of being awake I turned toward the coal fire that burned low on the opposite side of the room. My back was toward her when I heard her call out in an unusually sharp voice, "Who is that? Who—"

"It is I, Mama, Ellie. I wanted to show you—"

"Come here!" she commanded. "Let me look at you.

"You are not Ellie!" she hissed at me when I stood next to her bed. "How dare you pretend to be my daughter? Ellie could never bear to touch velvet! It made her skin crawl! You liar! You little beast! Get out, get out, get out!"

Her voice had risen as she excoriated me, and when she fell back on her pillows she was screaming like a soul in agony.

Nurse Hollis, Nellie, Madame, and the parlormaid all came running, the doctor was sent for, and I retreated to my room to wait for Mr. Lawrence to come home and tell me that I was no longer needed in the house on Colonnade Row.

❧

Darkness had fallen when Madame came to tell me that Dr. Ramsay had given Mrs.

Lawrence a sedative and that Mr. Lawrence would see me in the library at half past six. She noticed that I had changed my dress for a blue and gray striped surah and nodded in approval.

"I guess I won't be needed here any longer, Madame," I said, watching her straighten the quilt at the foot of my bed.

"Nor will I, *ma petite*," she said quietly. "But go now. It is time you went down to the library."

࿐

The smile with which Mr. Lawrence greeted me took me by surprise. During the long, gray hours of the afternoon I had naturally wondered what to expect for having failed him. I fully expected an angry dismissal and was almost reduced to tears when I saw the gentle smile on his face and the kindly look in his eyes.

"Sit down, my dear," he said quietly, "and please do not be upset. What happened was not your fault. In fact, no one is to blame. Neither Madame nor Nellie nor any of the rest of the staff knew of Ellie's aversion to velvet. Certainly I did not. She must have mentioned it to Flora, who, after all, supervised her wardrobe. They both loved clothes."

"Thank you, sir," I said, ready to cry with relief at not being blamed. "But I—I can't stay—"

"Wait, wait a minute. It is true that you cannot stay here, but if you think I am going to turn you out in the cold, Emily, think again. I have a plan, a plan that can be put into effect in a few days. My brother and I own a large house out in the country. We grew up there, grew up happily, and I think it would be a good place for you, at least for a while. Simon lives there now, and I would too if I could manage it. I love that place, and I think you'll like it. I'll see what arrangements I can make. In the meantime, stay away from Flora's room, and be quiet in the halls. She has been told that you have gone."

❧ · *Chapter VII* · ☙

I N SPITE OF Mr. Lawrence's comforting words, I was uneasy when I went to bed that night, and for the first time since I'd been there I was glad of the light that shone into my room from the gas fixture in the hall. Madame, who had emphasized the importance of fresh air and good ventilation, insisted that I leave my door open six inches when it was too rainy or windy to raise my sash. Ordinarily I would have closed my door and opened the window a crack, as Mama had always done.

I lay awake for some time, but after a while the sound of the rain drumming on the glass caused a comfortable drowsiness, and I was drifting off to steep when I became conscious of a change in the light in the room. I lay still, with my heart beginning to pound, as I watched the door slowly open wider and wider.

After a moment or two I was able to make

out the slender figure of Flora Lawrence. She was wearing the same peignoir I had seen on her as she rested on her chaise, and she carried something that looked like a ruler or a stick—the light was too bad for me to see it clearly. She approached the bed without making a sound, and through half-closed eyes I could see her looking down at me. Her expression—eyes glittering and mouth drawn back into a horrible grimace—frightened me so that I was unable to scream or call out, but when I saw her raise the stick or whatever it was in her hand, I rolled over to the far side of the bed and down onto the floor.

When I heard her moving around and realized that she was pulling the bedclothes apart, I crawled underneath the bed, thinking that she couldn't reach me there, and wondered if I shouldn't shout for Nellie or Madame. I didn't have to. When Mrs. Lawrence saw that the bed was empty, *she* began to scream, and the same series of piercing screams that the velvet dress had caused echoed through the house.

I heard the sound of running feet in the hall, and when the oil lamp on my dresser was lighted I peeked out from under the dust ruffle. Mr. Lawrence was holding his wife in his arms, while Nellie, Madame, and Nurse Hollis stood helplessly by. The three women were in their nightclothes, but Mr. Lawrence was still fully dressed. I guessed he'd had late callers again that night. The screaming had stopped, but Mrs. Lawrence was babbling something about having seen Ellie's ghost.

"A ghost, that's all she is. Ellie would never wear a velvet dress, but a ghost wouldn't know that. And there was no one in the bed. I knew she wasn't real, but I wanted to see if she would bleed. Ghosts don't bleed, you know."

"No, of course they don't," Mr. Lawrence said soothingly. "Flora, dear, let me take you—"

"No, no, no! Leave me alone! I want—"

"You want your own bed, don't you, dear?" Nurse Hollis asked. "And a nice warm drink to put you to sleep. Then you'll feel better."

I had to marvel at the nurse's patience with the irrational woman. She kept up a steady stream of quiet talk until Mrs. Lawrence calmed down and consented to let Nellie and Nurse Hollis lead her away.

Mr. Lawrence was standing in the middle of my room turning a silver dinner knife over and over in his hands when I emerged from under the bed.

"She must have taken it from her dinner tray and hidden it," he murmured and then gave a start when he saw me.

"Emily! My dear girl! Are you all right? She

could have cut your throat! She could have killed you! My God, she is surely mad! Are you sure you're all right? How on earth did you manage to get under the bed without Flora's seeing you?"

When I finished telling him what had happened, he shook his head and sank down on the love seat opposite my bed. "Things are worse than I ever imagined," he said as if to himself. "I can't send her away—she'd not last a day in an asylum—and Nurse Hollis can't be expected to—yes, that's it! I'll hire extra help, a nurse for night duty, and then Mrs. Hollis will just have to manage during the day."

He stood up suddenly and started for the door, but halfway there he paused. Turning, he asked if I would be afraid to go back to bed. I answered with more assurance than I felt that I would be perfectly all right and began to help Madame, who had been standing quietly by, straighten the bedclothes. After they both left I turned the key in the lock, and even though I left the oil lamp burning it was a long time before I slept.

Once again uncertainty about my future hung over me like the mist I'd seen hovering above

76

the river in the early morning when John Ireland and I were being rowed back to the dock. I was waiting for Mr. Lawrence to speak, to tell me more about sending me out to the house in the country, but for an entire week I saw nothing of him except at dinner, where he seemed hardly aware of my presence. He was unfailingly polite, and although there was nothing forbidding about him I didn't dare ask him when I was to go. Perhaps, I thought, the business about the night nurse is bothering him.

The first woman Dr. Ramsay sent over was dismissed almost at once; Mrs. Lawrence complained that she smelled bad. The second one left after one night, saying she would not take care of a violent person. Apparently Mrs. Lawrence had thrown a glass vase at her. The third one, a Mrs. Bundy, who came at eight in the evening and stayed until eight the following morning, was a heavyset, middle-aged woman who managed to please the invalid, although the rest of us didn't like her particularly. Cook objected to the midnight meal the nurse demanded, and Maggie, the chambermaid, said she was run off her feet providing clean linen for the sickroom. She reminded me of Mrs. Diebel.

"I think she takes 'em wiv 'er," I heard Maggie mutter when I met her in the hall with a pile of clean towels in her arms.

"No," Nellie said when I repeated Maggie's remark to her. "She can't be doing that. I keep count of all the linens, and there's nothing missing. God knows why she needs so many towels, though—so much laundry! But at least there's no more crying and screaming, and no more wandering around the house at night. We should be grateful for that." She was quiet for a moment, and then she said thoughtfully, "Of course it may be that Mrs. Bundy is simply determined to keep everything spotless in the sickroom."

We never did find out the reason for all the clean linen, but it wasn't long, maybe ten days or so, before we knew the reason for the peaceful nights. On a Tuesday morning just before Christmas, when Mrs. Bundy was leaving she told Nurse Hollis that the patient was still sleeping and should not be disturbed. Nurse Hollis nodded, glad of a chance to have a second cup of coffee in the upstairs sitting room where Madame was starting me on irregular French verbs. A little while later, while I was struggling with the subjunctive of *être*, she slipped out of the room, murmuring that she'd better check on Mrs. Lawrence.

Almost immediately she was back, ashen-faced, saying that we'd better send someone for Dr. Ramsay. I ran to find Nellie, who threw a

shawl around her shoulders and went to fetch
him herself.

༄

There were no more lessons that day. Mrs.
Lawrence's death from a massive dose of laudanum had, not surprisingly, brought the
household to a standstill. Nurse Hollis and the
doctor reasoned that either Mrs. Bundy had
been increasing the number of drops to ensure
a night's rest for herself as well as for the patient, or that the sick woman had helped herself
to the drug, which had been within easy reach
on the bedside table.

When questioned, Mrs. Bundy insisted that
she had never measured out more than the two
prescribed drops into the water in the medicine
glass, and Dr. Ramsay was inclined to believe
her since he'd used her satisfactorily on several
previous occasions. Nurse Hollis, however, reserved her decision. She had never, she said,
known Mrs. Lawrence to help herself to any of
the various medicaments that had been prescribed during her long illness.

"I know I am not to blame," Nurse Hollis
said just before she left Number 21 for good,
"but maybe I should have paid closer attention to the level in the laudanum bottle. But

she never took that during the day, just at bedtime. Poor woman! I can't believe she wanted to end it all. I'd rather think she woke up, saw Mrs. Bundy dozing in the chair, and simply helped herself to the laudanum. But we'll never know, will we?"

※

After the funeral Mr. Lawrence went away for almost a month, to visit his brother out on eastern Long Island, Nellie said, and while he was gone the old feeling of uncertainty, so familiar to me, seemed to spread through the entire household. We were all wondering what would happen next, and although I was fairly certain from what he'd said that he would provide for me in some way or other, the help had no such assurance on which to rely. Cook said she thought he might sell the house and take rooms in a hotel, Nellie wondered if he'd move out to the country with his brother, and Madame said she had no idea what he would do but she was thinking of going to live with her sister and give French lessons to girls of well-to-do families. Maggie, Maria, and Anna had no plans, but all three of them hoped to find positions, even if they weren't as nice as the ones they had on Colonnade Row.

"You could make a livin' sellin' yer pitchers, miss," Anna said, holding up a sketch I'd made of Cook standing next to the stove with a soup ladle in her hand. "Mebbe you'd get a dollar fer that one of the flowers. It's real purty."

Lately I'd been spending more time with my sketchbook in the afternoons, instead of curling up in front of the fire with a book. Sometimes I'd experiment with the little set of watercolor paints that Mr. Lawrence had given me after Madame showed him one of my drawings, and I was sitting in the kitchen window, trying to capture the irregular pattern of the snow on the garden wall, when he walked in unannounced.

Cook, startled, dropped the potato she was peeling, and Anna jumped up from her chair so quickly that it toppled over. Mr. Lawrence just smiled, helped right the chair, and said it was good to be home again. He patted the top of my head, and after glancing at my snow scene said that he liked it.

"We'll have to see about painting lessons for you, Emily," he said, patting my shoulder this time. "I think you have talent. Umm, something smells good, Cook. Will there be enough for me?"

"Indeed, sir, there will be. It's a nice capon I'm roastin'," she answered, picking up the basting spoon and opening the oven door.

I think I knew then that he had no intention

of sending any of us away, but many a time since that day I've wondered if it would not have been better, for me at least, if he had.

·*Chapter VIII*·

A S SOON AS he was able to arrange mat- ters, Mr. Lawrence adopted me legally, and from then on I was known as Emily Adair Lawrence. Over the years I grew almost as fond of him as I had been of John Ireland, but I could not bring myself to go on calling him Papa. I had hardly ever addressed him that way, but of course I'd had to refer to him as Papa when I was talking to Mrs. Lawrence. When I told him I'd have to call him something else I was afraid he'd be hurt, but he laughed and said he didn't blame me a bit.

"However, my dear Emily," he said, "you cannot possibly call me 'sir,' or 'Mr. Lawrence.' What shall we do?"

We finally settled on "Pa," which for some reason I didn't mind saying and to which he had no objection. My own father, of whom I had only the haziest memory, couldn't have been kinder than my adoptive one. Besides providing me with everything I needed and buying lavish presents for me (a silver pin in the shape of a kitten with tiny diamond eyes for my birthday, a real artist's easel for Christmas, things like that), he frequently took me about with him on the weekend. Sometimes we went to the Astor House for lunch, and occasionally to the Castle Garden for tea under a trellis, or else we might walk over to Broadway and Reade Street to visit A. T. Stewart's great white marble store with its domed rotunda and balcony where ladies of fashion often meet to see and be seen. Pa would invariably buy me some little "bauble," as he called it, the most delightful of which was a small music box that played "My Bonnie Lies Over the Ocean."

If I tried to thank him he'd put his hand gently over my mouth and tell me to hush.

"You are my daughter, my only daughter," he said one day, "and if I want to shower you with pretty things you will have to permit me. You see, I love you. But you know, you are becoming a beauty, my dear, and I shall have to be careful not to deck you out in jewels that will overshadow your natural loveliness."

I knew I looked nice, especially in the expensive clothes he provided for me, but as I studied myself in the mirror over my dressing table that night I wondered about "becoming a beauty." My deep blue eyes and dark brown, wavy hair were my best features, I thought, and my complexion was fair, but my nose seemed too short and my mouth too wide. I turned slightly away from the mirror in an effort to see my profile, but I couldn't manage more than a partial glimpse, so I gave up. I was just climbing into bed when I heard the doorbell ring, announcing the arrival of the usual night callers.

As the years went on I became more and more curious about those visitors, but something in Pa's manner kept me from questioning him about them. He'd explained that they were men who were too busy to see him during the daytime hours at the office, and I had to accept that, but still I wondered.

When I spoke to Nellie and Madame about the mysterious callers I learned nothing, or rather I did learn that there was something secretive, something we were not to inquire about, connected with the visits. Neither woman said exactly that, but I could tell from the manner in which they answered that if they knew what was going on they had no intention of telling me. Nellie said, "Oh, it's just business, Emily, and nothing for young girls to bother about." Madame agreed: "Mr. Lawrence has a right to his privacy, *ma petite,* and that is all there is to it.

Alors, ça suffit."

It was not too difficult for me to put the matter out of my mind. I was happy enough with things as they were, and shortly after my fourteenth birthday I was almost ecstatic when Pa sent me to art school and I had friends my own age. It wasn't really a school at all, merely a studio over on Canal Street, where Herr Anton Lubin gave lessons three afternoons a week to aspiring painters of all ages, or rather to anyone who could pay his fees.

We were a mixed group: one old man kept painting the same cathedral over and over again, and two middle-aged ladies painted nothing but flowers. The rest of us, four girls and three young men, were more adventurous, and although we worked hard at copying what-ever picture Herr Lubin set up in the front of the room, we seldom turned in a canvas that met with his approval.

"You call dat *ein Baum?*" he would shout, holding up what looked to me like a splendid picture of a tree with its leaves turning red and gold in the fall. "Dat is nossing but splotches of paint! Do it over!" And the student, whoever it was, would sigh and begin again.

I came in for my share of criticism, but by the time I'd been working with Herr Lubin for almost four years I had improved to the point where he occasionally complimented me. Not all of the students stayed as long as I did, but my three closest friends, all of them determined to become recognized artists, showed no desire to leave.

Of them all I liked Carrie Carberry the best, and I could tell that Pa approved of her when I brought her, along with Janie Randolph, Audrey Adams, and Millie Brewer, home with me after school for cocoa and cake.

"All four of those girls are suitable friends for you, Emily," he said after they left, "but Carrie Carberry is a cut above the others. I think she's more like you."

Oh, yes, he approved of Carrie, and after checking her address allowed me to visit her home on Great Jones Street, but right from the beginning he took a dislike to her brother. I didn't meet Hugh Carberry myself until I was seventeen—he'd been away at Harvard College whenever I'd visited Great Jones Street. I remember the first time I saw him: he created quite a stir the day he came to the studio to call for Carrie. I think Janie and Audrey were smitten by his good looks the moment he appeared—at least they talked about him constantly for the next few days and kept trying to make me admit that I had fallen in love with him on the spot.

"I wish I had your looks, Emily," Audrey moaned. "He kept watching you the whole time Carrie was getting ready to go."

I had certainly been conscious of his presence, but I deliberately refrained from doing more than glancing at the tall, elegant figure standing at ease near the entrance to the studio. By that time Herr Lubin had promoted me to portraiture, and I suddenly wanted to paint Hugh Carberry as he stood there partly framed by the doorway. I couldn't get the idea out of my mind, and that evening when I went up to my room I made a rough sketch of the picture I had in mind.

At first Hugh Carberry was seldom present when I went to visit Carrie; he was busy reading law, she said, when I asked her what his profession was. One day in the fall of 1858, however, he came in just as I was leaving and asked if he might see me home.

"Darkness comes early these days, Miss Lawrence," he said seriously, "and who knows what characters might be abroad in the dusk. Do permit me to see you safely home."

I did, of course, and after that he seemed to know when I would be at Great Jones Street. Carrie must have kept him informed. I, on the other hand, did not keep Pa informed. I said nothing to him about my friendship with

Hugh, and I was not exactly sure why I didn't. Perhaps it was because I was afraid he would not be pleased to hear that a young man he did not know was seeing me home. I'd better introduce Hugh to him, I thought, and decided to wait for an opportune moment.

As the season progressed our walks back to Colonnade Row took longer and longer, and several times we stopped for tea on the way. We talked, oh, how we talked! To my surprise Hugh had a genuine interest in painting and was familiar with many of the works of the great European artists, reproductions of which he'd come across in his father's library.

"Rembrandt's portraits come alive for me, Emily," he said one day when we were sitting in a small tearoom not far from Lafayette Street. "I think it's the subtle way he highlights the faces. How I'd love to see the originals someday!"

He paused for a moment or two, and then, looking over at me, said quietly, "If he painted you as you sit there now he'd make the most of the way the light from that window falls on your forehead." With that he leaned across the table and put his hand gently over mine, where it stayed, and might have stayed longer if the waitress had not appeared to ask if we needed more hot water.

After we left the tearoom and were making our way slowly toward Colonnade Row, the talk turned to books, and I asked him if he'd read *Uncle Tom's Cabin.*

"Yes, indeed," he answered. "A great book, that. And it will have far-reaching effects on the future of slavery. There's no doubt in my mind that it will have to be abolished, and I think it's just a question of time until it is. It should never have been allowed. Oh, here we are! You know, Emily, these walks are entirely too short. I'm going to have to map out a longer route, so that we don't have to stop in the middle of a conversation."

※

He did find a more roundabout way to Colonnade Row, but it still wasn't long enough to suit him—or me, for that matter. I have to smile when I remember the day the weather was so bad that Hugh hailed a cab and then complained to the driver that he was going too fast. When the cabbie slowed down to a walk, Hugh put his arm around me, and by the time he handed me out of the carriage at Number 21 I knew Janie and Audrey were right: I *was* in love with him.

"I'll pick you up at the studio at three on

Friday," he said earnestly as he escorted me across the pavement, "and we'll have a couple of hours together. Look at me, Emily. I love you, and I don't intend to let you go. Do you understand me?"

After that we had several wonderful Friday afternoons together. He wanted to hear all about my life, and I held nothing back, knowing instinctively that here was a man who expected complete honesty and would have no use for even a mild deception. He shook his head when I told him about Jack Hasty and Fat Sally, and when I finished the story of how Pa found me, what he wanted me for, and how he kept me on after Flora Lawrence died, he took my hand in his before speaking.

"Of course he wants to keep you, Emily; you are a precious jewel in his collection. But I am going to take you away from him as soon as I can. Will you have me?"

I couldn't speak. I could only smile and nod.

Later, when we were approaching Colonnade Row, he said anxiously, "You won't mind waiting, will you, love? It shouldn't be too long. And if I know you're there, nothing else matters."

"Oh, Hugh dearest," I cried. "Of course I'll wait—oh, I do love you!"

He drew me close to him as we came in

sight of Number 21 and kissed me until two little boys who lived in the neighborhood began to laugh.

We were radiantly happy for several weeks, seeing each other regularly on Fridays, and also on Sundays if Pa was out of town or too busy to take me out. What plans we made! And oh, such dreams! Then suddenly, everything changed. Pa had still not met Hugh, never even heard of him until he came unexpectedly one afternoon in early December to call for Carrie at our house. She and I had been up in my room, working on a design for a border we'd been told to make in imitation of those in medieval books of hours, when Maria came to tell us that Miss Carberry's brother was downstairs.

What was it that Pa disliked about Hugh? The moment I saw the cool, almost stern expression on his face instead of the warm, pleasant one I was used to I knew that for some reason he was displeased with whatever he'd had time to see in my lover before Carrie and I entered the drawing room.

It was an expression I had seen only once before, and that was when a red-faced man in a loud checked coat and bright green trousers had greeted him by name when we were walking up Broadway. How to describe it? Disdainful, contemptuous, or coldly indifferent? I

don't know exactly, but in any case it had startled me then, and when I saw the same look
turned on Hugh I gave an involuntary shiver.
At the time I had no way of knowing the real
reason for Pa's attitude, and I was totally un-
prepared for the truth when it finally emerged.

※

Pa said nothing to me about Hugh, and I decided that perhaps he'd had business affairs on
his mind and hadn't welcomed an interruption
just then. I studied his face as we sat on opposite sides of the fireplace after dinner and suddenly realized what it reminded me of: he bore
a striking resemblance to England's Charles the
Second as depicted in John Michael Wright's fa-
mous portrait, a copy of which hung in our
drawing room. Pa of course did not wear the
heavy, dark wig favored by the monarch, but his
own hair *was* dark brown, almost black, and
somewhat curly. The way his eyes were set in his
head, the straight nose, the longer than average
face, the sensuous mouth below the carefully
trimmed mustache made me think that given a
wig he could have posed for the portrait himself. The eyes in the painting dare one to approach the throne, but I had never seen that expression in Pa's eyes until the day he met Hugh.

They lit up now as he smiled across at me, any signs of ill temper erased from his face as he settled himself more comfortably in his chair. He was his usual charming self that evening, asking me about my painting, describing in detail an oriental chest he'd seen that day, and wondering if it wouldn't be a good thing for the two of us to spend a few days in Atlantic City later on, toward spring.

"I hear great things about the Chalfonte and Haddon Hall, Emily," he said, studying my face closely for any reaction. "They're said to be top-notch hotels, and I think we'd be comfortable there. It would be a nice change, and they say sea air is extraordinarily good for one. You might paint some seascapes, too. What do you think?"

"It sounds lovely, Pa, but do you think I ought to miss the art classes?"

"Oh, they don't matter—and Emily, did Madame tell you that she'd be leaving us? She said that now that you are eighteen you've outgrown her and that she's too old for governessing anyway. She'll go to live with her sister and have an occasional student."

Even though Madame had hinted as much from time to time, I hadn't taken her seriously. Now, faced with the reality of her going, I felt as if a dependable support had been pulled out from under me, and tears sprang into my eyes.

"There, there, Emily love," Pa said, springing up from his chair and sitting down next to me. "You'll see Madame at times, and you'll still have me, won't you, my dearest?"

He leaned over, put his arm around me, and drew me close to him. I wasn't comfortable, but when I tried to draw away he held me tighter for a moment before kissing me quickly on the forehead and releasing me.

ঈষ

Because the imminence of Madame's departure was uppermost in my mind, I didn't realize immediately the significance of Pa's behavior toward me. I couldn't help but notice, however, that he shaved off his mustache.

"I don't know whether I look better without it, my dear, but I feel better," he said and looked pleased when I commented that I thought he looked younger without it.

No, I was not very alert just then, but by the time the Christmas festivities were over, I could no longer ignore the signals he was sending, which became more pronounced after my governess left.

I sorely missed her comfortable, and comforting, presence more than I would have thought possible. She'd always been there to answer my questions, to explain the changes that took place in my body, to see me through the minor illnesses I'd contracted over the years, and even to instruct me in the mysteries of married life.

"For you will marry, *ma petite*," she said with a smile. "With a face like that there is no doubt about it. And I must say that there is nothing quite so pathetic as a young girl getting into the marriage bed and expecting to sleep quietly beside her husband."

Also under her tutelage I had become adept at holding my own in conversation, at entering a room without seeming gauche, at wearing clothes suitable to the occasion—in fact, Madame "finished" me. She was, she said as she kissed me good-bye, satisfied with her work.

"No tears, *ma petite*," she said, putting her arm around me. "It is not as if we will not see each other ever again. Mr. Lawrence has assured me that he will permit you to visit me and my sister at our little house on Church Street, Number 42 it is, and as soon as I am well situated there I shall send you an invitation to take tea with us."

I did go to "take tea," or more often chocolate, with her and Mlle. Jeanette, the bonnet maker, several times (but never on a Friday) over the next months. The little house on Church

Street looked to me like a bit of France, Paris perhaps, transported to New York with its Louis Quinze chairs and Madame Récamier sofa. Everything was delicate and light in those small rooms, and I had to wonder if the two aging ladies who lived there didn't dress to complement the furniture, or whether their laces and brocades were reminiscent of fashions they'd known when they were girls in France.

Their father, I learned, had been a successful *avocat* who had been forced to leave France for political reasons (these were never explained to me) when Madame and her sister were young.

"He and my mother brought some of their treasures with them, you see," Madame said, gesturing toward the Sèvres vases on the mantelpiece, "and as much of the furniture as they could. Papa always thought of this house as a temporary home and was convinced he would be able to provide for us a grand mansion in a few years."

She paused for a moment and smiled ruefully. "But that never came about. I do not know why. So when he and our mother died I became a governess—that is when I decided to be Madame Fortier instead of Mademoiselle— and Jeanette became a *modiste*. Papa did, however, leave us this house and the furnishings he had loved."

"This is indeed a charming room, Madame," I said, "especially the soft colors in the tapestry on the chairs and in the velvet of the draperies."

"Ah, yes," she said, pouring more *chocolat* into the dainty porcelain cup on the marqueterie table next to my chair. "They have worn well over the years. Papa knew quality when he saw it, as I believe you do, *ma petite.* Come, try on this little hat Jeanette has just finished. I think it will suit you."

¿ß

Madame's room had been the one next to mine, and the first thing Pa did after she left was have it made over into a studio for me, with a connecting door cut in the wall common to the two rooms. By the end of January no trace of Madame remained. The flowered wallpaper was replaced with pale ivory paint, the rosy carpet was removed, revealing the warm tones of the hardwood floor, and where chests and dressing table had stood against the walls, shelves had been installed to hold my paints and canvases.

It was all splendid, and I was so glad to have a place of my own, where I could work undisturbed, that I was slow to realize that Pa's plan was to put an end to my days with Herr Lubin and my friends. I didn't think he knew about the times I spent with Hugh.

He went about it slowly at first, dropping little remarks about the bad weather, the draftiness of the studio on Canal Street, or the danger of picking up a cold or a cough from one of the students. Then one day early in February he came right out with it.

"Don't you find you can paint better here than at the school, my dear?" he asked when he stopped in on a Saturday morning to watch me working on some illustrations for a child's book that Herr Lubin had asked me to do. "No distractions, no trudging through the wet streets. Perhaps it is time you gave up that school. Yes, I believe so. I shall notify Herr Lubin on Monday that you will no longer need instruction."

"But, Pa—"

"No, no, my dear. My mind is made up. I can see how splendidly you work on your own—I love to come in here and watch you. And, Emily, my love, I want you to be safe, safe from the danger of illness—the city is filled with consumptives and others with highly contagious diseases—and safe from outside influences. Now that Madame is no longer here to supervise you, I must take over."

I was too stunned to argue with him, and after he left for the office I sat with idle hands and racing thoughts. Did this mean I would be cut off from Carrie and the others—and from Hugh? Would I never walk home from the studio again with Hugh bending his face toward me as he held my arm? Would I spend my days here in the room Pa had renovated, with him coming in at all hours to watch me paint, never going out unless he accompanied me? That's how it sounded. I shuddered as I realized in a sudden flash that there was something unnatural in this new attitude toward me, that despite the more than twenty-year difference in our ages he was beginning to look upon me not as a daughter but as a replacement for poor Flora Lawrence.

The increasing number of caresses, the good-night kisses, the frequent embraces, to all of which I had paid little attention in the past, now took on a different, and unpleasant, meaning, and I was suddenly nauseated at the thought of any further physical contact with the man who had rescued me from poverty, the man who had introduced me to a way of life I would otherwise have never known.

ぱ

Perhaps I am mistaken, I thought, as I prepared

for bed a few nights later after a delightful dinner at the St. Nicholas Hotel on Broadway and Spring Street, the hotel Mr. Dickens had called "the lordliest caravansari of them all." The meal had been superb, and Pa was at his best, attentive without overdoing it, never touching me unnecessarily, and simply calling a cheerful good night to me before going into the library. I'll talk to him tomorrow, I decided, and make it clear that I do not want to lose my friends. If I go about it the right way, pleading loneliness, maybe he'll understand. And I needn't mention Hugh.

I never had a chance to speak to him again. When I awoke the next morning the house was silent, and Pa was lying on the floor of the library with a length of rope twisted around his neck.

⁌ · *Chapter IX* · ⁌

AFTER ONE LOOK at the bulging eyes that stared vacantly upward, I covered my face with my hands and sank down into the leather armchair where I had so often curled up with a book taken from the shelves that lined three of the room's walls. I knew I should do something, call for help, notify the authorities, or sound the alarm that murder had been done, but I remained frozen in position for I don't know how long.

At some point I was aware of a persistent tapping, as if someone were knocking on a wooden door a short distance from where I sat. I listened for a moment; in the silence that surrounded me and the dead man the sound was unnaturally clear. Why was everything else so quiet? Why weren't the maids about? Where was Cook? Was I alone in the house with a corpse? I stood up, and as I glanced around the room, carefully keeping my eyes averted from Pa's body, I saw that several volumes had been pulled from the shelves behind the desk, revealing the open door of a small safe that had been built into the wall. It seemed to be empty, and I thought that Pa must have been killed because he surprised the thieves.

The tapping continued, and moving quietly, I traced it down the hall to the kitchen, then to the broom closet in a corner near the back door. Like the other closets and cupboards this one had a latch on the outside that snapped into place when one closed the door, making it impossible to open it from the inside. I was looking around for something to use as a weapon when I heard a smothered cry that sounded like "Dear God in heaven" and realized that the voice was that of Anna, the kitchen maid.

"Oh, oh, oh miss! Oh, miss," she sobbed, clutching my hands when I released her. "Oh, miss, thank God you're safe! The murderers! The cowardly ninnies. Oh!"

"Anna, stop!" I commanded. "Stop at once! Quiet down, and tell me slowly—"

"Yes, miss, yes, miss, I will. But I need my tea," she said, still crying as she turned to pick up the kettle.

"Anna, what happened to Mr. Lawrence?

Where's Cook? Where are Maria and Maggie? And Nellie?"

"Gone, miss. Gone . . ."

"Gone where?"

"Just gone, miss. Oh, awful it was!" She began to cry even harder.

It took the better part of an hour and several cups of strong tea before the poor frightened girl was able to tell me what she knew. Apparently the maids, Cook, and Nellie had just finished clearing up after celebrating Maggie's birthday with cake and coffee and had started up to their rooms by means of the back stairs when they heard Mr. Lawrence cry out.

"We all stood still, miss," Anna said, looking fearfully around the kitchen, "and then Mr. Lawrence comes out of the library and tells us not to worry, he just dropped his strongbox on his foot and it hurt, but nothin' was broke."

"Then did you go upstairs, Anna?"

"Yes, miss. An' Maggie and me was talkin' when Cook came in an' said she wanted us all to go downstairs with her—she was afraid of somethin'—to see if Mr. Lawrence needed any-thin'. She didn't like the way he looked, she said. So we all went down, quiet like, an' that's when we saw him, lyin' there wiv 'is eyes starin' out of 'is head."

She started to cry again, and when she

calmed down I asked her if anyone had come to see him last night.

"Must have, miss, but we never seen nobody. Then when Cook seen the master on the floor, she said she was leavin' an' that we'd better go, too, else we might be blamed. And Nellie an' Maggie an' Maria said they wasn't stayin' where there was killin' either, even if it was the middle of the night.

"They all run to git their things, but I was too scared—I thought the men that did it would be waitin' outside to murder us all—so I ran and hid in the broom closet. I didn't know as I'd be locked in. Anyway, where would I run to? The others, they all knows somebody. Oh, miss, what'll we do?" she wailed.

"Why didn't someone go for the police?" I asked.

"I told you—they was all scared they'd be blamed and put in prison!"

"Anna, do you have any idea who these men were?" I asked. "Do you think they're the ones who came before?"

"Musta been, miss. Once I seen one of 'em carryin' a bag, a black bag it looked like, and one time I heard Cook tellin' Nellie that when the men came at night they had black bags with 'em. Cook said there was money and diamonds in them bags, but 'ow could she know? She never seen inter the bags."

"No, she couldn't have known, Anna," I said. "And now I'd better send for the police. I'll go—"

"No, miss! Now we'd better git outta here! Them men might come back an'—ow! They're comin' now! That's the front door openin'!"

She would have darted back into the broom closet if I hadn't held on to her with one hand while I picked up one of the black iron stove lids with the other. We stood perfectly still and listened to the footsteps that came steadily down the hall toward us. My heart was pounding furiously as I heard them pause for a moment in front of the library door before continuing on in our direction. I don't know whom I expected to see, but never in the wildest flight of fancy would I have been prepared for the man who finally stood in the doorway.

He looked so much like Pa that I could do nothing but stare stupidly at him, speechless and frightened. He was clean-shaven and had a bloodstained plaster just below his right eye, but he had the same dark eyes, the same curly black hair (although Pa wore his without a part and curled slightly over his ears), the same slightly elongated King Charles face, and the same well-formed, sensual mouth. The clothes were not Pa's, though; they were more tweedy and outdoorsy than anything he would have worn. Nevertheless, the resemblance was striking enough to give one pause.

"You must be Emily," the man said in a voice that could have belonged to John Lawrence. "My God! You do resemble Flora! John told me about you, about how you looked like Ellie, too. I'm his brother, Simon, his twin brother, actually. What were you going to do with that thing?" he asked, pointing to the stove lid. "Hit me over the head with it? I already have one wound on my face."

"I didn't know who you were, sir," I answered haltingly, wondering how he could sound so complacent after just having seen his brother lying dead in the library.

"Well, you know now, Emily, and you mustn't be frightened of me. The last time John came out to Grape Island he said that if anything happened to him I was to take care of you, and I shall respect his wishes, even though we didn't always get along."

"What happened to Pa, sir? Who killed—"

"Name's Simon, Emily. None of this 'sir' business, please. As for John, let us say he used poor judgment, made bad decisions, and angered the wrong people. He had to answer for it, but he didn't deserve to be killed."

He paused for a few moments and looked

away, as if he was realizing for the first time that it was his brother who was dead. Then he continued: "The police have been notified. They will see that justice is done."

"I don't understand—"

"Nor need you understand, at least not at present. Sometime in the future I may explain the whole business to you. Right now it is imperative that I get you out of here before anything else happens. Go pack your clothes and whatever else you need. We have a long trip ahead of us."

At this point Anna let out such a loud wail of despair that Simon Lawrence and I both jumped.

"What the devil's the matter with you?" he asked sharply.

"P-p-please, sir," she stammered through her tears, "p-please, kin I go with Miss Emily? I got no place!" She covered her face with her hands and rocked back and forth, the picture of misery.

"She's a good girl, sir—I mean Simon," I said quickly, putting my arm around Anna's drooping shoulders. "She really is. Even Pa said so."

"Kitchen work?" he asked. "Cooking? Cleaning?"

"Oh, yes, sir," Anna said, brightening up immediately. "Cookin', laundry, everythin', sir. I'll pack my duds." And before either of us could say anything further she had flung open the door to the back stairs and was hurrying up to her room.

"Well," Simon said with a rueful smile, "I guess we're taking her along. Who knows? She might be an asset. I had a woman coming over from the mainland by the day, but last week she went off to Rhode Island with her husband. He wanted to try the fishing there. What's this one's name, anyway?"

༄

Later on I had to wonder why I acquiesced so readily in Simon Lawrence's plan to leave Colonnade Row so precipitously for Grape Island, a place about which I knew nothing. I should certainly have tried to send a message to Hugh, or even Carrie, but I wasn't thinking straight. Perhaps I was relieved that someone—anyone—was taking charge of things that awful morning, but looking back I realize how immature, almost childlike, I still was. Simon's resemblance to Pa may have had something to do with it, and his authoritative manner did not encourage questions or suggestions.

༄

"We'll take the ferry across the river to

Brooklyn," Simon said when I came downstairs half an hour later with my satchels and the handbag Pa had bought me the week before, "and we should be in time for the Greenport train at one o'clock."

He must have seen the question in my eyes as I glanced back toward the door of the library, for he leaned over and patted my shoulder before he spoke.

"Don't worry about John, Emily. I've arranged for the body to be sent out to Grape Island. He'll be buried in the cemetery where Lawrences have been buried for almost two centuries, ever since the first John Lawrence died. He was the one to whom the king of England gave the island by royal grant."

"How on earth did you have time to arrange—"

"Plenty of time," he interrupted. "I was staying in the city, in John Street, last night, and word came to me about five o'clock this morning. The details need not concern you. Unfortunately, various affairs—one of which became somewhat rough and accounts for the plaster on my face—kept me from coming here any sooner. Come, the cab is waiting to take us to the ferry. Where's that girl? Oh, there she is. Come along, both of you." And picking up two bags he had evidently left in the front hall he

111

ushered us into the street.

"Were you and Pa in the same import business?" I asked when we were settled in the cab.

"Emily, for God's sake stop calling him Pa! You make me feel as if he's—was—my father instead of my brother. Can't you say John?" he asked crossly.

"Yes, if you like," I answered meekly. "Were you partners with—John?"

"You might say that, but he always thought of himself as the one in charge, the boss, because he was all of half an hour older than me."

I remembered that he'd said he and Pa didn't always get along, and now from the edge of bitterness in his voice I wondered if he had even liked him. It did not seem wise to continue the conversation in the direction it had taken, and after smiling encouragingly at Anna I sat back and occupied my thoughts with the letters I would write to Hugh and Carrie Carberry.

※

The trip in the train seemed endless, and by the time we arrived, cold and tired, at the little station in Mattituck, darkness had fallen. An ancient carriage drawn by two tired-looking horses took us along narrow, snow-covered roads to a dock, where we piled into a small boat—a wherry, Simon called it—manned by a heavyset fisherman. Anna clung to me as the waves of the incoming tide caused the boat to rock. I knew it was coming in from what John Ireland had told me about the motion of the water on one of our East River trips, so I put my arm around her and reassured her as much as I could. I would have welcomed a supporting arm myself, Hugh's, and his shoulder to lean against.

"Leave your bags on the dock," Simon directed after we had clambered out of the wherry, "and I'll send someone down to collect them. It's only a short walk up to the house, and by the time you've had something hot to eat and drink your things will be there. By the way, Emily, and you, too, Anna, I do not propose to say anything about John's death tonight. I'll find an appropriate time tomorrow or the next day. Understand?"

I thought he was probably too tired to undertake any explanations that night and wanted time to think over what he would say to whatever people were up at the house. After all, he had had a long and arduous day.

Simon found a lantern in a shack on the dock, and with his free hand he held it up so that we could see a few feet ahead of us in what seemed like solid darkness. I didn't see the house until, slipping and sliding on the icy

113

crust of the snow, we were almost on top of it. Suddenly a dog barked, and almost immediately a door swung open, causing light to stream out on the snow that had been trampled down around the entrance. A burly fellow in workman's clothes held an oil lamp in one hand while he restrained a nervous Irish setter with the other.

"All right, Sham, all right," Simon called as we negotiated the last slippery steps. "Don't be frightened, Emily. That's only Shamrock, a completely useless animal but a great pet."

"Shammy's not useless, Papa!" a child's voice cried out indignantly. "She caught a rabbit today, and Josh's gonna cook it."

By that time we were inside a kitchen so large that the light from the fireplace and a few oil lamps left the outer edges and corners in darkness. A little boy, whose age I judged to be five or six, hurled himself at Simon, who swung him up in his arms and hugged him before introducing us to the other occupants of the room.

"Papa!" the child exclaimed. "You've cut your face. Did you fall down?"

"Yes, son," Simon answered. "I took quite a tumble, slipped on an icy step and banged my head against an iron railing. It's healing up now but may leave a scar. Remember how you cut your forehead when you fell off the swing?"

"That hurt," the little boy said, nodding his head. "Does your cut hurt?"

"A bit, not much," Simon said, putting him down and turning to the rest of us.

Besides the fellow who let us in I saw an elderly woman in a rocking chair in front of the fireplace and a young man with hair as red as the dog's pelt standing near the coal range. These three remained silent, content to stare at Anna and me with a mixture of surprise and suspicion in their eyes.

The old lady, Simon said, looking at her affectionately, was his Aunt Becky.

"She brought us up, John and me, didn't you, Aunt?"

The woman nodded but said nothing while she continued to inspect the newcomers.

"And that big fella there is Bill Penny, my right-hand man. Billy, run down to the dock and pick up the bags and things we left there. They'll be needed tonight. Here, take this lantern. And over there by the stove, that's Josh Norton, who, among other things, cooks for us. And this young one here is my son, Paul.

"Good news for you, Josh—I've brought you some kitchen help. Her name is Anna. And this young lady is my brother's adopted daughter, Emily Lawrence, come to stay with us."

"Why is Johnnie's daughter here?" asked his

aunt in a clear, pleasant voice. "And where is he?"

"I'll tell you later, Auntie. What we need now is something hot. Got any soup there, Josh? Take your wraps off, girls, and sit down. Paulie, help me drag some chairs over to the fire."

The rest of the evening is rather a blur in my mind, but I do remember eating the hot soup that was more like a stew and drinking a large cup of strong tea before Simon showed us the way upstairs and pointed out two adjacent bedrooms to us. The last thing I recall before falling asleep is Anna creeping into bed with me, saying something about being afraid of the dog.

❧ · *Chapter X* · ❧

"**H**OW COME THEY had the beds all ready for
us, Miss Emily?" Anna asked the next
morning when we were awakened by the
smell of bacon frying. "Clean linen an' all?"

"I don't know, Anna. Maybe the woman
who came over from the mainland to work for
Simon kept them ready. Don't you remember
Nellie saying that a guest room should always
be in order?"

"Oh, yes, miss. I remember that, but out
here's a long way for guests to come—all that
water. Are we gonna be here long, miss? Have we
come to stay? An' will there be other guests?"

Some of those same questions had occurred
to me, but at the time I had no answers. I can
see now that the shock of Pa's death had had a
numbing effect on my mind, leaving me un-
willing, or unable, to do anything but follow
Simon's orders. It was so much easier to let

someone else see that I was housed, fed, and clothed than to make the effort to support myself. And Simon, who had been so kind, and looked so much like Pa, seemed to have assumed full responsibility for my welfare.

"Who would the other guests be, miss?" Anna repeated.

"We'll find out," I answered finally. "But come now, I smell breakfast cooking."

❧

Ten days later Pa's coffin arrived. Simon had it carried into the parlor where it rested on two chairs while the grave was dug in the partially frozen ground. When the time came for us to follow the farm wagon bearing all that remained of the man who had for more than eight years made himself responsible for me, I suddenly realized the enormity of the debt I owed him.

I knew that had he lived I never could have given him the love he looked for, but on that bright winter morning as we made our way through the woods, my heart overflowed with gratitude.

Simon read the burial service, and as Josh and Billy began to shovel the dirt back into the grave, Aunt Becky, who had remained seated in the wagon during the brief ceremony, suddenly cried out, and the only tears shed for John Lawrence flowed down over her soft old face.

⁂

By the end of my second week away from New York I had a fairly good idea of what life on a privately owned island in the Sound was like, at least during the winter months, and while I did not dislike what I saw and experienced, I knew from the beginning that I would never feel completely at home in such surroundings. The Lawrence house, a comfortable two-story wooden structure dating back to the early eighteenth century and facing the narrow dirt road that traced a route around the island, was well preserved and well appointed for all its isolation, but something was missing. . . .

The barn and outbuildings on the other side of the road were of little interest to me, but Anna liked to go with young Paul to watch Bill Penny milk the cows and to collect fresh eggs in the chicken coop. She wouldn't go near the horses, though, saying they reminded her of Miss Ellie's death.

The house was surprisingly comfortable on those cold, damp winter days. Each room had a fireplace, and the wood baskets that Josh

Norton filled each morning held a full day's supply of logs. On the ground floor was a little-used front parlor with faded brocades and velvets, and next to it was what had once been the dining room but was now Aunt Becky's bedroom, since the rheumatism in her legs made it difficult for her to climb the stairs. Both rooms opened off a center hall, on the other side of which were Simon's office and an informal sitting room that Paul had pretty much taken over for his toys and games.

The kitchen area, I was told, had been added sixty or seventy years ago and could be reached either from Aunt Becky's room or from the rear of the center hall. Where the original kitchen had been no one seemed to know or care. The house had two staircases, a wide, gracefully curved one in the front hall and a steep one going up from the kitchen to three cell-like rooms, obviously meant for servants, where Bill Penny and Josh Norton slept. Simon had laughed at the apprehensive expression on Anna's face when he showed us the back stairs and quickly said that that part of the house was for men only.

The four main bedrooms on the second floor opened off the upstairs hall, Simon's and Paul's on one side and Anna's and mine on the other. To the rear and down a narrow passage, four smaller but nicely furnished bedrooms were ready for any influx of guests. Simon said they were seldom used now but that in the old days his parents and grandparents entertained lavishly, especially during the summer months.

⚜

The heat from the fireplaces was frequently not strong enough to warm an entire room, and it didn't take Anna long to see to it that hot bricks wrapped in flannel were put in our beds at night. Nor did it take her long to establish herself as chief cook, much to Josh Norton's relief. She giggled when I expressed surprise at her ability to turn out a meal, a good meal, with so little practice.

"An' what do you think I was doin' all the time I spent with Cook in the city house, Miss Emily?" she asked. "Sure I was only kitchen maid, but I couldn't help it if I listened, could I? An' many's the time Cook would say, 'Anna, my back's so bad today, will you beat up this cake for me?' An' one thing led to another, it did. So you see, miss, I learned to cook, an' a good thing, too, from the looks of things here. Take a peek at them pots—filthy they were till I showed Josh how to scour 'em."

In a remarkably short time she had Josh

obeying her every command, and it did not take any great perspicacity on the part of an observer to realize that the young man was torn between resentment at being ordered around and fascination with this somewhat waspish girl.

When I saw Simon smile one evening while he listened to a slight altercation between the two as we sat by the fire with Aunt Becky, waiting for the evening meal, I asked him how Josh happened to be living on the island.

"As soon as the weather warms up a bit I'll have him working outdoors," he said, leaning over to put another log on the fire. "But to answer your question: about three, no, four years ago he ran away from where he lived over near Sag Harbor—he was fifteen or sixteen then. Apparently it was a terrible home, a filthy shack, no mother, a drunken father about as bad as you could find around here. I saw him fishing off the Mattituck dock one day and asked him to help me load supplies onto our wherry. Well, he did, he did it willingly, and as we talked I found out that he had no place to stay, so I took him on. Nice boy, good worker—"

"Tell her about Bill Penny, Simon," Aunt Becky interrupted with a little chuckle.

"Auntie loves that story, Emily," Simon said, smiling across at the old lady as he stretched out his legs. "And it's a good one. It's rather hard to believe, though, when you consider the size of Billy and his strength. He's one of the strongest men I've ever known, and yet he's terrified of a little old lady not even as big as you are, Emily."

"Why on earth—" I began.

"Wait. About ten years ago he used to do odd jobs over on the mainland in and around New Suffolk. He's not too bright, but he's a good worker. He lived at Widow Kiley's boardinghouse, and in return for his room and board he kept the place up, fixed the roof, tended fires, all the things a handyman would do. Everything was fine until one day the widow told him to stop what he was doing and pick strawberries—she wanted to make a pie for supper. Bill tried to tell her there weren't enough ripe ones yet, but she insisted there were and said not to come back without them.

"Well, he took a pail out to the patch, and sure enough he could find only a handful of red ones. He knew the widow would be angry, and he had a healthy respect for her temper. He was wondering what to do when he remembered that when he was younger he and some other boys used to raid Miss Acker's patch, which was just down the road a bit. Now, Miss Acker was the schoolteacher, rather a fierce one, and the youngsters used to dare each other to put even one foot on her property. She and the widow had been on the outs for years, hadn't spoken to each other since the night at a church supper when they got into an argument about how to make green tomato pickle relish.

"Billy generally steered clear of Miss Acker, but he thought she'd be in the schoolhouse that morning—he forgot it was Saturday—and climbed over the fence into her yard. He was bending over, looking for berries, when suddenly there was a bang, and something whizzed past him. He dropped the pail, berries and all, and just had time to see Miss Acker raise her shotgun again before he took off. I found out later it wasn't much of a weapon, just a popgun she kept to shoot pellets at the rabbits she'd see in her garden, but Billy didn't know that.

"He made straight for the water—it wasn't more than a hundred yards off—with Miss Acker right behind him, and even after he dove in she took a couple of shots at him. He says he stayed underwater until his breath gave out and then kept swimming until he got to Grape Island. I found him up in a tree down near our dock, watching to see if she was coming after him in a boat. He's been here ever since, says he never got over being scared of Miss Acker after she rapped him over the knuckles with a ferrule when he was a schoolboy."

"Remember how Johnnie used to laugh at that story, Simon?" Aunt Becky asked. "He'd get Billy to tell it almost every time he came out here. Of course he knew Miss Acker; he used to sell her fish when he was a boy."

"Surely Billy has outgrown his fear by this time, hasn't he?" I asked.

"I guess not, Emily," Simon answered. "Miss Acker's still alive, must be over eighty by now, but he still shivers when her name is mentioned. Says he won't set foot on the mainland until she's in her grave, and maybe not then."

"I used to see Miss Acker from time to time," Aunt Becky said after a moment or two. "If I met her in the grocery store she'd invite me to have a cup of tea with her. Worst tea in the world, brewed from herbs she raised in her garden. Awful stuff. Most times she'd ask me about Billy, but of course I never let on that he lived here. She'd laugh, that cackle of hers, when she told how he dove into the water. Ah, here's Billy now, and Paulie and that silly dog."

Shamrock bounded across the kitchen to have her head rubbed by each one of us before settling down with a thump on the hearthrug, young Paul told us Billy had let him feed the chickens and asked me if I would draw a picture of his favorite rooster for him, and Anna sent Josh over to say supper was ready. It was all so cozy, warm, and comfortable that I wished I felt happier than I did. But what, I kept asking myself, what on earth am I doing here? And what comes next? Oh, if I could only see Hugh!

⁓· *Chapter XI* ·⁓

Grape Island
Mattituck, Long Island
February 4, 1859

Dear Carrie,

You will probably have learned from the newspapers that my father (my adoptive father) was killed last month, and you will have been wondering what happened to me. His brother, Simon (my uncle by adoption?), brought me out here to Grape Island so that I would be out of harm's way. It all happened so quickly that there was no time for me to get in touch with you before we left.

I will write a longer letter soon. Please be assured that I am well and reasonably happy.

With all good wishes to you and your family, I am

Your art school friend,
Emily Lawrence

Grape Island,
Mattituck, Long Island
February 20, 1859

Dear Carrie,

I was happy, more than happy, I was over-joyed to receive your letter and the one from Hugh. How excited he sounds at the prospect of spending three months in London as an aide to one of the partners! I am sure the firm will be pleased with his work, and I know that you and your parents are very, very proud of him. His future looks bright indeed.

I will do my best to answer your questions, but first let me say that I miss you both and look forward to a reunion sometime—but I know not when. I can make no plans at the moment, for I don't know just where I stand. Simon is reluctant to speak of the future. I have the impression that he is quite content to let things go on as they are now, but that is not to my liking. He is not a particularly happy man, and for that reason I have hesitated to initiate a discussion of my position, my financial status, and my future. But I simply cannot spend the rest of my life on Grape Island, and if I don't broach the subject Simon will probably assume that this is what I want. I shall have to speak up soon.

You asked about my painting. Unfortunately I have no canvases here—I had to leave the ones that Pa bought me in New York—but Simon says he will bring me some when he makes his next trip to the city. He travels there at least once a month. Until then I shall have to be content with my sketchbook, which I carry with me on my walks.

Paul, Simon's six-year-old son, begged me to draw him a picture of his favorite rooster, and now he wants one of Shamrock, the Irish setter. What would Herr Lubin say if he knew I was busy with animal portraiture? Of course I am not limiting myself to the birds and the beasts. Aunt Becky, an elderly woman who brought up both Pa and Simon, was so pleased with the sketch I did of her that she persuaded Josh, our handyman and jack-of-all-trades, to make a wooden frame for it.

Write to me soon, Carrie. Your letters are *so* welcome!

Affectionately,
Emily

I couldn't tell Carrie how much more welcome Hugh's letters were than hers, but they were—love letters, all of them. A shiver of pure happiness clutched at my heart each time I reread them in the privacy of my room. They stopped coming, though, shortly after he arrived in England. I thought perhaps he was too involved in legal work.

After I addressed my letter to Carrie I put my pen away and stared out the window at the light rain as I turned my thoughts to the conversation I'd had with Aunt Becky the previous day. She was watching me struggle with the pair of mittens I was trying, under Anna's intermittent supervision, to knit for Paul, when she suddenly looked across the kitchen to where the boy was playing with Shamrock.

"That child needs a mother," she murmured softly, folding her hands and sitting up straighter in the rocking chair.

Her remark gave me the opening I'd been waiting for, and I asked, as gently as I could, what had happened to Simon's wife.

The old lady closed her eyes for a moment before saying in a whisper, "She went away."

She was quiet for so long I thought she'd gone to sleep—she did doze off from time to time—but then she opened her eyes and leaned forward toward me.

"She went away," she repeated in a scarcely audible voice, "and then one time she came back. She didn't stay long. She said she'd just come to see Paulie—he was about a year old then—and after a few days, maybe a week, she left. She didn't even say good-bye to Simon.

Not that he cared."

"Where do you think she went?" I asked.

"Oh, back to that fisherman she'd run off with, I s'pose," she answered. "She must've gone to him, because it wasn't long, maybe a month or six weeks, when they were both drowned. Their bodies were washed up on the shore over near Greenport. Simon was sent for to identify her. She was still his wife, you see."

"How did they know she was married to Simon?"

"Oh, my dear Emily, people in these parts know everything that goes on," she answered with a disapproving shake of her head. "Bunch of gossips they are, the men as bad as the women. Not that Simon cared a hoot about what they thought. He'd never loved her, only married her because he'd gotten her into the family way one night when he'd had a bit too much to drink. And he'd been drinking trying to forget Flora. You'd think he'd have got over her by that time. She'd been gone, Flora had, some eight, nine, ten, I don't know how many years. I've lost track of time, my dear.

"Anyway, that's where Paul came from. I'm just glad he favors his father in his looks, and not that Lily Cutts. There! I finally remembered her name! She tricked Simon into marrying her, but she wasn't happy, and neither was he. Flora was his only love, the love of his life until she died, that is. Then Simon seemed to put it all behind him. Sad, isn't it?"

She sat quietly, hands folded in her lap while she rocked gently and watched the flickering of the fire. She looked as if she were considering what to say next, and when she finally turned back to me she spoke slowly.

"Yes, poor Simon. First Johnnie took Flora away from him, then got him mixed up in this import business. They were such good, wholesome boys while they were growing, up until the time Johnnie left for the city. He should have stayed here, made Grape Island his home. Look what the city did to him—killed him! That's what it did, the city and the people he associated with."

"Who were these people, Aunt Becky?" I asked.

"I never saw them, but I wouldn't be surprised if they were unsavory characters. Once in a while when Johnnie came out here I'd hear him and Simon talking. They'd sit here in the kitchen after I'd gone to bed, and I could hear snatches of what they were saying—something about when the men would come to be paid, I remember that. Oh, they never should have been in that import business! It's not safe. I hope now that Johnnie's gone Simon will let it

132

go. He was always the more sensible one."

She probably would have gone on talking, but just then the kitchen door burst open, and Anna came in with Paul and the basket of eggs they'd collected that morning.

▪

Poor Simon, I thought, as I folded my letter to Carrie and put it in an envelope, he must have loved Flora as much as Pa did. No wonder he sounds bitter about his brother from time to time. Could he have been the one to—? No, by no stretch of the imagination could I picture the gentle, easygoing man who ran this strange household resorting to such violence. And yet . . . he'd been at the house in Colonnade Row so soon, so promptly after Pa had been killed, saying he'd heard about the murder at about five o'clock in the morning. Who could have told him? The murderer himself? Then he must know who did it. . . . Oh, why hadn't I asked more questions at the time? I had simply, stupidly, accepted what Simon told me: that Pa had made mistakes, miscalculations, and had to pay for them. Perhaps Pa had refused to pay the men who came to the house.

I sat watching the rain for some time, mulling over what I had heard from Aunt

Becky and wondering what action, if any, I should take. By the time Paul shouted up the stairs that supper was ready, however, I had decided that the first thing for me to do was to let Simon know, as politely and firmly as I could, that I wanted to return to New York and continue to study painting. I would have to wait for the right moment, though, and under no circumstances would I tell him that I wanted to be in the city when Hugh returned from England.

Feeling assured that everything would work out in due course, I hurried downstairs in time to see Anna taking a pan of corn bread out of the oven. It smelled heavenly.

⁂· Chapter XII ·⁂

A S A RESULT of my frequent walks, sometimes with Paul or Anna, but always with Shamrock, I had the geography of what I now considered my temporary home pretty well fixed in my mind. I did not often leave the narrow road that loosely encircled the island, since I was timid about venturing into the deep woods in the central part, although Billy assured me that the only danger I might encounter there would be entanglement in the vines of the wild grapes from which the island took its name.

I particularly liked to wander along the rocky shore on the western side, from which the views of the Sound were spectacular. Simon brought me the promised canvases from the city, Josh made me an easel of sorts, and once the snow was gone and the temperature had moderated I was able to spend a couple of hours on a fine day trying to capture the ever-changing beauty of sea and sky beyond the rugged promontory that jutted out into the water.

Closer to the shore a cove that was almost hidden from casual observance interested me, or rather, challenged me to transfer to my canvas the peaceful and yet sinister mood it evoked, almost as if light and dark were contesting for supremacy in this small, uninhabited area.

Opposite the grassy bluff where I set up my easel the promontory stretched out into the bright blue of the Sound against a background of clouds and sky, while directly beneath me the shaded water of the cove lapped gently against boulders that looked as if they had been hurled at the shore. No little sandy beach softened the cruel edges of the cove, and yet, in spite of the rocks and a suggestion of a threat lurking in the deep water that barely rippled in the early spring breeze, an aura of peace and quiet was almost palpable. At least it was that day.

What would it be like on a stormy night? I wondered. Would waves rush in from the Sound, causing the calm waters of the cove to rise in turmoil and dash themselves against the rocks? Or did storms bypass this secluded spot? Was it protected in some mysterious way by safeguards that it had built up over the centuries? Who could tell me? Simon, I thought, as

I packed up my finished painting. I was anxious to show it to him—he'd seemed interested in my work—but now I wonder if I would have been so eager to display that particular painting if I had known that it would, indirectly perhaps, lead me to question the apparent innocence of life on Grape Island.

಄

Until the night that Simon saw my picture of the cove it had never occurred to me that our existence on this out-of-the-way piece of land was any different from that of scores of others who lived in rural areas. I believed what Simon had told me about his having business affairs in New York, affairs related to his partnership with Pa, and I assumed that the income derived from the sale of imported objects was sufficient to keep his household and dependents in the relative comfort in which we lived. He spoke no more about the source of his money than Pa ever had, and except for the brief monthly trips to the city, he devoted his time to us and to overseeing his property. Once the snow disappeared he spent the greater part of the day out of doors with Billy and Josh, mending fences, repairing leaks in the old barn, and in general keeping the place shipshape.

Since he was so busily occupied all day, I decided the best time to show him the painting would be during the evening after the others had gone to bed, when the two of us would sit for a while by the fire and talk over the events of the day. I knew it was the best thing I'd done, and I intended to use it as proof that I was serious about further study, but Simon's reaction was so contrary to what I'd expected that all thoughts of artistic advancement were driven from my mind.

"Is this the latest landscape?" he asked, smiling as he held out his hands to take the picture from me. "Ah, let's see it."

Without warning the smile vanished and his face darkened. As he studied the painting, turning it this way and that to catch the light, he pressed his lips together until they formed a thin line and frowned as if he were looking at something disagreeable.

"Don't you like it, Simon?" I asked, puzzled by the sudden change in his expression.

"Hmmm—oh, yes, yes," he answered absently. "It's very nice, but . . ."

"But what? Simon, what's wrong with it? Don't you like the colors? Or is it the mood?"

"Oh, no! The colors are fine. It's just—it's just that that cove is so hidden away—"

"That's just it!" I exclaimed. "That's what

makes it so special. And that's the title of the painting: *The Hidden Cove*."

"Yes," he said softly. "*Hidden Cove*, that's its name all right. But Emily, I had no idea you were wandering around down there."

"Why not?" I asked. "It's a beautiful spot, one of the loveliest on the island."

"Beautiful, maybe, but also dangerous. Keep away from there, Emily. It's not safe. People have been known to drown there."

"People! What people, Simon? Who else ever lived here besides the Lawrences?"

"Oh, in the past," he said vaguely. "I've heard stories about how some of my ancestors came to grief there. Then there was a boating party when my grandparents were entertaining some special guests, two of whom lost their lives."

"Well, you can rest easy, then," I said lightly, "because I have no intention of doing any boating there or anyplace else. I do want to paint the cove from another viewpoint, though—"

"No! No, Emily!" He did not raise his voice, but he spoke so forcibly that I jumped nervously.

"I don't understand—" I began.

"Well, you will just have to take my word for it that it is not a safe place for you. You are not to go there again, and that's an order. Do you understand me now?"

My pride would not let me respond. I merely stared at him, and after a moment he turned to bank the fire for the night.

It was definitely not the time to tell him I wanted to leave Grape Island.

⸘

The sudden change in Simon's ordinarily warm, pleasant manner might have frightened me if I hadn't been so perplexed. That night, when sleep was a long time coming, I went over our conversation in my mind and wondered why he was so concerned about my safety. Was he worried that Paul might follow me and fall off the bluff? Or was it something else entirely? Had the picture reminded him of some other disaster, one more recent than the boating accident and one for which he was responsible, financially responsible?

No, I thought, that didn't seem too likely. Never once had I heard him complain about the expenses involved in "keeping the place up," as he put it. Nor did I ever hear him refuse to buy whatever Aunt Becky or the rest of us requested when he and Josh made the weekly trip to the mainland for supplies. I think if I'd asked him to bring me a gold bracelet he would have

140

come back with it.

In a way, Simon's complacent attitude toward expenditures concerned me. Did he, I wondered, have a practically inexhaustible supply of money? If so, where had this wealth come from? Had Pa left him a fortune? Could their partnership in the import business have been so vastly remunerative?

I knew I couldn't put any of those questions to Simon, and in truth I didn't really need to know the answers. What I *did* need to know was whether he would advance me enough money to live on while I made a start on a career as an artist. Then, as soon as my pictures began to sell, I would be in a position to repay him. My common sense told me that I would be well advised to stay where I was, right there on Grape Island, at least until Hugh came back from England. But is that what I wanted? No, not really.

❧ · *Chapter XIII* · ❧

ARLY THE NEXT morning I awoke with a start when Anna burst into my room with the news that Aunt Becky had taken ill during the night.

"She's askin' for you, miss. Told me to wake you up. Poor old soul, she doesn't half know what she's sayin'."

"Where's Simon, Anna?" I asked as I hurriedly put on my dressing gown and found my slippers.

"Gone for the doctor, miss. Took Josh and went out as soon as it was light. Not that it'll do much good."

One look at Aunt Becky's wrinkled face, pale and drawn against the pillows, convinced me that Anna was right. She opened her eyes when I spoke her name, and held her thin, almost transparent hand out to me.

"Anna, find some brandy," I whispered before kneeling down at the side of the bed. I had suddenly remembered how John Ireland had held a small glass of that restorative to my mother's lips when she had a particularly bad spell. "Whether it does any good or not I don't know," he'd say, "but I do know it can't do any harm. Besides, it tastes good."

As Anna left the room Aunt Becky tugged at my hand, indicating that I should come closer to her. My face was almost touching hers before she tried to speak. Her mouth worked silently for a moment or two, and then with an effort that was painful to watch, she whispered, "Go away, child, go away."

"Away from the island, Aunt Becky?"

Almost imperceptibly she nodded. "Get away while you can," she continued. "They'll be starting up again. Take Anna with you." She coughed, and I slipped my arm around her shoulders to raise her head a little. "Billy and Josh," she went on, "they'll be all right, but it's no place for young girls."

Anna returned with a medicine glass of brandy at that point, and the old lady managed a few sips while I supported her head.

"What is it, Aunt Becky?" I asked when Anna had gone back to the kitchen. "What will be starting up again?"

"The men," she whispered. "The men come

by boat. As soon as the weather's good they come. I wanted to tell you sooner. Don't wait, child—I'm not sure about Simon. . . ."

"Tell me," I urged. "Tell me what Simon has to do with the men!"

She tried to speak again, but the effort was too great for her failing strength. I think I heard her say "Go" once more, but that was all. She kept her eyes on me, and as I watched, her shallow breathing became steadily weaker until finally it ceased.

❦

An hour later Simon returned with Dr. Simpkins, who said he was surprised that Aunt Becky lasted as long as she did.

"Weak chest she had, Simon," he said. "Had it for most of her life, but you took good care of her. A cold or congestion in the lungs could have carried her off at any time. I see it happen every spring in the old ones."

He gently closed Aunt Becky's eyes and pulled the sheet up over her face before turning to Simon.

"You'll miss her, eh? Brought you and Johnnie up after your parents went—what'd they die of, anyhow?"

"Cholera," Simon answered. "They'd gone to

New York to celebrate their seventh wedding anniversary and never came back—except to be buried. Johnnie and I were not quite six, and from then on Aunt Becky took over. It's hard for me to remember a time when she wasn't here."

He stood looking down at the bed, and I was about to leave the room when he turned to Josh and asked him to row Dr. Simpkins back to the mainland. As they started for the door it took all my self-control not to go with them, not to cry out: Wait! Wait for me! Aunt Becky said I should go!

&

Later that morning Simon called Anna and me into his office, where he was seated at the old rolltop desk against the wall, with some of Aunt Becky's papers in front of him. I knew they were hers—that spidery handwriting could belong to no one else in the house. He may have seen my glance, or he may have merely wanted to keep the papers from being blown about by the slight breeze from the open window to his left, but in any case he carefully placed a large ledger on top of them before turning to us.

"Josh and Billy will make the coffin," he said, "and the burial will be tomorrow morning in the old cemetery. See if you two can lay her out. Put her into that blue dress with the lace collar that she was so fond of and fix her hair. Oh, yes, and sprinkle some of her dried lavender around, for God's sake."

Fortunately Anna knew what to do, and as we worked she kept up a running monologue about how when so-and-so died in her old rooming house she didn't have a decent stitch to be laid out in.

"An' but for Bessie Malden bringin' down an old skirt and shirtwaist she'd've gone out of this world the way she came into it," she said, straightening up and looking down at Aunt Becky's now peaceful face. "There, miss, she'll do real fine. When the boys have the coffin ready we'll put some pillows in it and lift her in real careful."

۞

Simon did not go into deep mourning for Aunt Becky, but for several days after her death he was quieter than usual, and his face looked drawn, as if he wasn't sleeping well. There were new lines around his eyes, and the scar on his cheek from the wound he'd received on the night of Pa's murder was more prominent than usual. At the end of a week, however, he began to seem more like his old self. He surprised us all by announcing at breakfast that he wanted us to get to work clearing out Aunt Becky's furniture from her room so that we could have a proper dining room. No one questioned his order, but I couldn't help wondering when such a room would ever be used.

Billy and Josh dismantled the bed and carried it, along with the dresser and washstand, up to the attic. Anna and I removed the few articles of clothing from the armoire before that, too, went up, and Simon checked the contents of the drawers and pigeonholes in the small desk in the corner of the room.

When only the faded oriental rug remained, and the room had been aired, swept, and dusted, handsome pieces of dining room furniture (Chippendale, I think) were brought down and set in place. When Simon heaved a sigh of relief as Josh carried Aunt Becky's commode upstairs I must have looked puzzled, for he took me aside and said softly, "I'm not doing this to rid myself of memories of Aunt Becky, Emily. I loved her. It's just that having a bedroom, particularly an empty one, just inside the front door—well, I find it distasteful. Especially one with a commode in full view. Besides, you and I may dine here some night by candlelight, like real gentry."

That remark, I realized later, sounded more like Pa than like the Simon I had come to know.

·*Chapter XIV*·

"ILL WE BE eatin' in the dinin' room now, Mr. Simon?" Anna asked as she placed a platter of bacon and eggs on the table the next morning. "If I could find the proper cloth an' all—"

"Only on special occasions, Anna," he interrupted, helping himself to a piece of buttered toast. "This will do for the present. The main thing, the important thing, is that now the room looks the way it was meant to look, a gracious, properly furnished one, so that if we have company you can set us up in there. There's plenty of table linen in the drawers of the sideboard, and I'll have Billy bring down the barrels of good china. That will all have to be washed, and then you and Emily can arrange it in the china cabinet."

Was he trying to keep me busy? Was I to be a helper around the house, a sort of glorified housekeeper? Did he think I would be content to spend my days seeing to the laundry, ordering the meals, and keeping him company in the evenings? A vision of myself in the years to come flashed across my mind, an Emily grown old, sitting in Aunt Becky's rocking chair, sleeping in her bed, which had once again been brought down from the attic. I knew I wouldn't let that happen, but I was suddenly so angry with Simon that my coffee cup clattered when I put it down. I saw the surprised look on Anna's face, but Simon didn't notice; he was too busy giving Billy instructions about fixing a wheel on the farm wagon.

"There's a loose spoke on one of the rear wheels," he was saying. "It needs replacing. And I want you to test the rest of them. See if the tailgate needs reinforcing, too. And do it today, understand?"

"Can I help Billy, Papa?" Paul asked eagerly, "and can we go for a ride in the wagon when we're done?"

"Later, son, later," Simon answered. "Right now I think your time would be better spent with some lessons. You will be going to school over on the mainland in the fall, you know, and it might be a good idea if you had a head start. Emily has been reading to you, and that's a help, but it would be better if she took you in hand and taught you to read by yourself. A couple of hours a day should do it."

Paul looked puzzled, but he didn't say anything. Neither did I just then, but half an hour later, when I knocked on the door of Simon's study, I had my speech prepared. He looked surprised when I closed the door behind me, sat down in the chair next to his desk, and paused before speaking.

"Yes, Emily, what is it?" he asked impatiently. "Can't it wait? I'm extremely busy."

"This won't take long, Simon," I said quietly, "and I hope you won't misunderstand me. I am sure you know that I am truly grateful to you for taking me in—"

"I had no choice, my dear. I'd promised John—"

"I know that, and I don't know what I would have done if you hadn't. But Simon, I can't go on living here."

"Why ever not?" he asked sharply. "You are well taken care of."

"Yes, of course I am, but it's not the sort of life I want. I want to go back to the city, to study painting, to learn all I can about it. Also, I want to be with my friends."

"And, if I may ask, where would you live and how would you support yourself?"

"I was hoping you'd advance me enough to get started. Oh, I'd pay it back—"

"My dear Emily, how do you expect to earn

151

any reasonable sum of money? Your little pictures are very nice, but have you any idea how much they are worth? A pittance, perhaps."

"I don't know what they are worth, but I'll find out. And Simon, I've been meaning to ask you, didn't Pa leave me anything in his will?"

"Everything came to me, my dear. His share of the business, his house—which, incidentally, I have sold along with all of its contents. Put this absurd idea out of your head. Grape Island is your home. And now that Aunt Becky is no longer with us, you are the mistress here. I am very fond of you, Emily dear. I'll even marry you if you think that will make you happy. Well, don't look so surprised. Think it over, and we'll talk about it when I return. I must prepare to leave for New York on the afternoon train. With John gone, the city end of the business falls on me, and I'll be gone for two, possibly three, days. Anything you want me to bring you?"

I simply stared at him, feeling my face flush with embarrassment and rage at his casual, disinterested offer of marriage.

"No, Simon," I said as calmly as I could, and stood up to leave. "Not a thing."

છ

After he left I called Shamrock and walked

slowly along the narrow dirt road with no destination in mind. I have only two or three days, I thought, to devise a way of leaving Grape Island before he returns. Money was the problem, money for train fare and for food and lodging when I reached the city—where was it to be found? I knew that Simon had plenty, all of Pa's wealth as well as his own, and for a few minutes I considered searching his office while he was away. Suppose I found some. Would I take it? Would I steal? If I took it with the intention of paying it back, would that constitute a crime? Fat Sally would have sneered at such scrupulosity, I thought, and shuddered at the very thought of the woman.

"You ain't cold on a day like this, are you, Miss Emily?" Josh had come around a bend in the road so suddenly that I was momentarily startled. "Walk over here in the sun. It's warmer."

"Did you row Mr. Simon across, Josh?" I asked, falling into step beside him.

"Yep," he answered. "Mostly he rows himself over and leaves the boat on t' other side for when he comes back. I dunno why it's different this time."

"Maybe he thought we might need something from the general store while he's away. He can always get someone from the town dock to row him back, can't he?"

"I guess so," Josh said, frowning. "But I think he's gettin' ready for another—hey, lookit that there robin! Never saw one this early. Must mean warm weather comin'."

"Josh, what were you going to say about Simon getting ready for something?" I asked quickly.

"Oh, nothin', miss. Look, I gotta hurry up. Billy'll be needin' help with them wheels."

He loped off to the barn, leaving me to follow more slowly and to wonder what Simon might be "gettin' ready" for. Perhaps the company he hinted we might be having? A lot I care about his company, I thought. I just care about leaving here. As soon as I returned to the house I went up to my room and took stock of my possessions, wondering which ones I could sell. The little cat pin with the diamond eyes should be worth something, but to whom? If I could only find enough for the train fare I could ask the Carberrys to put me up for a few days while I looked for work. If Hugh were back from England—my heart gave a little lurch at the memory of the look in his eyes the last time I saw him—he would help me. I knew he would. But it was too soon; he couldn't be back yet.

Maybe when Simon comes back he'll change his mind, I thought, putting away my jewelry. Perhaps if his business goes well he'll be in a better mood and try to see things my way. If not, I'll leave anyway. I'll take Anna with me; maybe she has enough for the train. I know he's been paying her wages.

The next day was so lovely and warm, an April day for the poets to celebrate, that I packed up my painting things and in spite of Simon's injunction set off for the cove. I walked past the knoll on which I had formerly set up my easel, to a spot that gave me a better view of the promontory, and set to work. Shamrock, who had followed me, or at times led me, was lying half asleep in a sunny spot nearby, and aside from the faint lapping of the water on the rocks no sound could be heard. I worked steadily, trying to catch the shadows in the clefts of the rocks before the turning of the earth on its axis caused them to change. I was so lost in what I was doing that I didn't hear Billy's footsteps until he was almost next to me, peering over my shoulder.

"That's real nice, Miss Emily," he said, pointing to the painting. "Real nice."

"Thank you, Billy," I said. "I'm glad you like it. But aren't you supposed to be working? Didn't Simon—"

"Well, the wagon's ready. Nothin' much more to do until milkin' time. I like to come down here, 'specially when it's quiet like this, not when . . ." His voice trailed off.

"Not when what?"

"Not when there's a shipment," he answered, looking out over the water.

"A shipment? What kind of shipment?"

"Money, mostly," he said, pulling up a blade of grass and putting it in his mouth. "Sometimes jools. All spring and summer they'll come. Weather's too tricky in winter."

"Billy, what are you talking about? Who comes?"

"Why, the men, Miss Emily. I thought you knowed all about them."

"No, I don't. What men?"

"Why, the men from the city as has the money an' the jools. They works for Mr. Simon. That's why he has to go to the city, to make sure they're workin'. They stores things up over the winter, and when there's too much for Mr. Simon to bring down on the train they come out with it in the boat. Bring it right in here to the cove. That's deep water, you know."

I suddenly remembered the two bags Simon carried with him the day Anna and I left Pa's house. "And what does Simon do with the shipment?" I asked after a moment.

"Don't rightly know, miss. But I think he puts the money in the bank, the jools, I dunno.

Some boxes he puts in the barn. I dunno what's in them, but sometimes he takes them over to the mainland. They can't all be jools—they're too heavy."

"You knew Mr. John Lawrence, didn't you, Billy?" I asked.

"Oh, yes, miss. He useta be here now an' then. Him and Mr. Simon was partners, like. But he stayed in the city mostly, and when he was alive Mr. Simon didn't go there so much as he does now."

"When is the next shipment coming, Billy?"

"Anytime, miss. Mebbe tonight, mebbe tomorrer night. Midnight he said he'd be on the boat. Told me so. About midnight, he said, either today or tomorrer. 'Be there with the wagon both nights,' he said."

"Be where? Here?"

"That's right, miss. Right here."

"And the men who come in the boat, do they come up to the house?"

"Na. They sleep on the boat until the tide is right, then they take it back to the city."

"Then they are not the company he was talking about," I said thoughtfully.

"Oh, no, miss. Dunno who that is. Mebbe someone from the bank."

While Billy was revealing this surprising and alarming secret of Simon's—and of Pa's (although I'm sure he didn't realize he was doing it)—the sky had begun to cloud over, and a sudden, chilly wind had sprung up. I put my brushes and paints away, all interest in the picture I had started with such enthusiasm lost. Billy picked up my easel, and together we started down the path to the dirt road. I half expected him to regret what he'd told me, but nothing of the sort happened. He whistled for Shamrock and then trudged along beside me, rather like a pet dog himself.

"Hurry, Miss Emily," he said suddenly. "We're gonna have one of them hard rains pretty soon."

He was right. The sky had lowered since we left the cove, but my thoughts had been so occupied with what he'd said about Simon's and Pa's activities that I'd paid little attention to the change in the weather. Shamrock raced ahead of us, and when the first large drops of rain spattered down through the overhanging branches, Billy grasped my hand, forcing me to run awkwardly beside him, with my paint box banging against my hip.

The barn was closer than the house, and when we burst in through the wide door, wet and out of breath, Josh stood up from behind the wagon and frowned.

"Whyn't you finish the job?" he growled at

Billy, paying no attention to me. "That tailgate was so loose—"

"It latched, didn't it?" countered Billy.

"Yeah, it latched all right, but one good jolt on that bumpy road and it would've come undone in a hurry, and then where'd the boxes be? An' Mr. Simon—"

"Never mind that, Josh. What else we gotta do? Sweep out the wagon an' lay the rug down in it?"

"Yeah, an' in this weather we'll need the canvas cover, too. You know how partickler he is."

The two of them seemed to have forgotten me completely, and when they set to work I wandered off to other parts of the old building, casting my eyes around for any sign of the boxes Billy had mentioned. I was staring up at the ladder that led to the hayloft when Paul came running over from the house saying Anna wanted six eggs.

"She's gonna make a cake, Emily," he panted, "an' I'm to help. Wanna watch me find the eggs?"

⁂

Shortly after supper that night I went up to my room after telling Anna I had a headache and would go to bed early. The afternoon shower had passed, and from my window I could see the moon, almost full, rising slowly over the treetops.

That will help, I said to myself as I changed into a woolen skirt and the heavy sweater Anna and Aunt Becky had knitted for me. I don't dare take a lantern, I thought. I don't want to be seen; I just want to *see*.

I waited until I saw signs of activity across the road and heard the wagon come out of the barn before I went quietly down the stairs and slipped out through the kitchen door. Billy had told me that the distance from the house to the cove was a little less than a mile, and on a fine morning it seemed like no more than a short stroll, but in the dark, even with the moon shining down from a clear sky, the route seemed endless. I kept close to the bushes and undergrowth at the side of the road, tripping only two or three times over a stone or a fallen branch, being as quiet as I possibly could.

I heard the horse whinny before I saw the wagon and stood still for a moment or two before going on. I knew there was a large boulder just to one side of the knoll where I'd set up my easel, and slowly, ever so slowly, I inched my way up the wet slope toward it. Once I had crouched down behind the big stone, I could peer out from over the top or from either side without, I hoped, being seen. Occasionally I heard Josh and Billy speaking in low voices, but I couldn't see them. I did, however, have an unobstructed view of the cove itself, so I settled down to wait and watch for whatever happened next.

Every so often I was forced to change my position. The spot I had chosen was rough and uneven, strewn with bits of broken stone. I knelt until my knees ached, then tried crouching with both hands braced against the boulder—an untenable position—and finally sat down, regardless of the damage to my skirt.

Fear of dislodging a pebble, stepping on a twig, or exposing my presence in some other way made shifting my position a dangerous undertaking, or so I thought at the time. Josh and Billy were not particularly intelligent, but they were accustomed to the island and familiar with its sounds, whereas I was not, and most important of all, they were only a stone's throw away from my hiding place.

I could see the lantern that hung from the back of the wagon, probably from the mended tailgate, but the two young men were in darkness and were so quiet that after a while I wondered if they had gone to sleep. Only the flicker of the lantern and the changing patterns of the moonlight on the water kept me from giving in to an unreasonable fear of being left alone in a world that would otherwise have been shrouded in unrelieved darkness. How strange, I thought, that the moon and the lantern, two such disparate objects over which I had no control, should provide me with the assurance I needed in order to do what I had set out to do.

Suddenly two things happened to rouse me from the reverie into which I had fallen: in the woods behind me a night bird flew from one tree to another, calling raucously to its mate, and a light appeared some distance out in the Sound.

Billy and Josh went into action at once, covering and uncovering the lantern in what I took to be signals to the approaching boat. After that things happened quickly. Gruff male voices shouted orders as the boat negotiated the entrance to the cove and sailed quietly closer to the shore than I would have thought possible. Some sort of wide board or gangplank was brought out, and in no time at all it was secured to the boat's side at one end and then made to fit neatly into a spot between two rocks at the other (evidently this had been done many times before), where Billy pounded it firmly into position.

"Easy there, Billy!" Simon's voice was sharp as he stepped confidently along the plank. He was carrying a bag or satchel in one hand and something I couldn't see clearly in the other— it could have been another bag.

"Move the wagon closer!" he shouted. "Here, Josh, take these, and Billy, get ready to help them unload. Work quickly, now! They're sailing back tonight and don't want to miss the tide."

Two men followed him onto the shore, each carrying what looked like wooden boxes tied around with rope. Simon stayed on land supervising Josh in the loading of the wagon, while Billy hurried back and forth across the plank. As the men passed in and out of the swath of light cast by the ship's lantern, I could see that the shorter of the two, a stout fellow, was dressed like a seaman in dark trousers and a heavy sweater, while his taller companion wore a long black coat and, incongruously, a top hat.

After watching the operation for a few minutes longer, I decided I had seen enough to satisfy my curiosity, enough so that I could confront Simon with my knowledge of his strange activities the next day. I prepared to leave my hiding place at once—I wanted to be back in my bed before they returned—but a glance at the new position of the wagon told me that there was no way I could get to the road without being seen. I would simply have to wait until they left and then rely on their going first to the barn to unload before going to the house. In that case, I could follow them at a safe distance and make my way undetected around to the kitchen door.

After what seemed like an endless wait but probably was no more than half an hour, I heard the top-hatted man say, "This here's the last one, Simon," and then the three of them stood on the shore talking for a few minutes. Finally Simon climbed into the wagon with Josh and Billy, and they drove slowly down the path to the road. I saw the bareheaded man cross the plank and go inside the cabin just as the wagon disappeared into the darkness, and in my desire not to be too far behind it I left my hiding place too soon.

I had forgotten two things: one, that the man in the top hat was still on shore, and two, that the slope behind me consisted of ledge rock covered with a slimy green growth. Without warning, my feet shot out in front of me, and when I tried to get up I slipped again and rolled to the bottom of the slope.

When I looked up, the man in the top hat was staring down at me and calling to his companion to come and see what he found.

"Doakes! Come here! Gimme a hand!" he shouted, and as I struggled to my feet he grasped my arms firmly with strong hands.

"Wot in hell is she doin' here?" Doakes asked. "Who is she? Simon's woman?"

"Not now she ain't," came the reply. "She's mine."

"Let go of me!" I cried. "I live here!"

"Not anymore you don't," the tall man said. "You're comin' with us. Got a rope, Doakes? Good. Tie her hands behind her back."

"What'll you do with her, Jack?" Doakes asked, pulling the rope tight around my wrists.

"Never you mind. Get her on board."

"But Jack, bad luck to have a woman on board. You know that."

"Shut up, Doakes, and do as I say. Get her on board."

I made a desperate effort to wrench myself away from the hold Doakes had on me, but the tall man grabbed me by the hair, and as I looked up into his face I knew that he was Jack Hasty, the same Jack Hasty who had let his wife sell me and my dress to Fat Sally for two dollars eight years earlier.

·Chapter XV·

ANY ATTEMPT TO escape from those two men at that point would have been futile; either one could have picked me up like a feather and carried me aboard. So with Jack Hasty's large hand gripping my arm I walked, unprotesting, across the plank and onto the boat.

"How'd ya find 'er, Jack?" Doakes asked once the three of us were on board.

"Almost stepped on her. I'd gone off a little way to relieve myself, and when I came back there she was, lyin' on the ground. She'll talk, don't worry."

"Why are we takin' 'er?" Doakes whined. "I tell ya it's bad luck—"

"Shut up, Doakes, and get that anchor up. The tide's turning. You, girl, get in the cabin, and don't touch nothin', hear?"

I stumbled over a raised threshold as he

pushed me into the cabin, which was lighted by a smaller lantern than the one they'd hung on the deck. When my eyes adjusted to the dimness I could see two bunks, each made up with a pillow and blanket, a small stove with a pipe going up through the roof, an upright chest of some sort with a large padlock on the handle, and a couple of stools. I couldn't imagine what it was I was not supposed to touch—the stove? the lantern? And how could I touch anything with my hands tied behind my back?

Bone weary and close to tears, I sat on one of the bunks and then lay down. The pillow was surprisingly soft.

❧

When I awoke Jack Hasty was sitting on a stool near the stove, drinking from a battered metal cup. He stared at me for a moment and then asked gruffly if I would like some coffee.

"I would, but how can I drink it?" I asked petulantly.

He gave a short laugh, more of a snort, really, and told me to stand up so that he could undo the knots in the rope. My arms were stiff and my wrists felt sore, but I managed to hold the mug he filled for me and drink the hot, strong coffee without spilling it. I said I was

168

hungry, and without a word he unlocked the chest and brought out some bread and cheese. For a moment I was transported back to the day of John Ireland's death, to waking up in Jack Hasty's house and being given bread and cheese by his daughter. What other repetitions would there be? I wondered. Would he sell me to Fat Sally again?

He watched me eat, not saying anything. I had a feeling he was waiting for me either to ask questions or to volunteer information about Simon. I didn't think he had recognized me—after all, it had been eight years since he'd seen me, and then only briefly—and until I had some inkling of his plan for me I thought it best to keep quiet.

"You can't go nowhere," he said, standing up and looking down at me, "unless you want to swim, and it's a long way to any shore. So I won't tie you up again. Stay put here in the cabin. Go back to sleep if you like."

After he left I did lie down again, this time with the blanket pulled up over me, and I was almost asleep when I heard voices out on the deck. Doakes and Hasty must have assumed I was out of earshot because they freely discussed their participation in Simon's operation, speculating on how much he would pay them when he returned to the city—what Pa had paid them, I supposed. It was a somewhat dis-

jointed conversation, but this is what I remember hearing:

HASTY: He'll pay to get the girl back—if I
           decide to let her go, that is.

DOAKES: Ya shoulda left 'er there, Jack.

HASTY: No, sir. You can't tell what she
           might have done, or how much
           she knows. Where'd we be if she
           went to the police and tole them
           what she seen? *If* she knew what
           was goin' on.

DOAKES: So what'll you do with 'er?

HASTY: Don't know yet. Wait for Simon,
           mebbe. Or get her to talk. See
           how much she cottoned to.
           Somethin' about her seems like I
           seen her before.

DOAKES: Not a bad-lookin' girl.

HASTY: Now, don't you get any ideas,
           Doakes. She belongs to me, and I
           don't want no trouble from you.
           From Simon, neither.

DOAKES: I didn't mean nothin', Jack.

HASTY: Well, see that you don't. An'
           shut up now, I'm tryin' to
           remember somethin'.

Their voices grew faint as they moved to
some other part of the deck. I climbed out of

the bunk, and after straightening the blanket and plumping up the pillow I sat down next to the stove. I had just become aware of a change in the motion of the boat when Hasty came back into the cabin. He glanced first at me and then at the bunk before pulling up the other stool so that he could sit facing me. He looked as if he were about to begin to question me, and in order to forestall that I asked what kind of boat we were in.

"She's an oysterman, or rather, an oyster sloop," he answered in the same conversational tone I had used. "Single mast, small cabin, once used for harvesting oysters up and down the coast. Simon and his brother bought it cheap from the family of an oysterman who drowned."

"Is she oceangoing?" I asked, trying to keep the conversation going.

"Some might say so, I wouldn't," he replied, stretching out his legs. "Not strong enough for rough weather. That's why we're anchored here in Duck's Bay right now. Little squall comin' up."

I was about to ask for something more to eat when he suddenly leaned forward and stared at me. "How well do you know Simon?" he asked abruptly.

"Simon?" I asked, looking at him blankly.

"Yes, Simon," he said crossly. "What were

you doin' on his island?"

"I—he asked me to marry him."

"He did, did he? Hmmm. And what did you say? Yes? No?"

"I didn't answer. I told him I'd see. But I don't want to marry him. I want to go to New York."

"New York, eh? Well, you're on your way there now, girl, and there you'll stay until he comes to fetch you. An' believe me, he'll pay a pretty price for you. He owes me plenty. Hey, why're you lookin' at me like that?"

"I was wondering why you always wear a top hat," I answered evenly. "It's supposed to be worn only on formal occasions."

"It is, is it?" he growled. "I'll wear it when it suits me, dammit. An' though it ain't none of your business, I'll tell you this much: this hat has charmed my life, brought me luck. And besides, I like it."

He must be stupid, I thought, as he went over to the large chest and busied himself with its contents for a few minutes. Maybe it won't be too hard to get away from him.

"We'll eat now," he said, handing me a brown earthenware bowl of beans mixed with chunks of meat. I managed to eat all of the beans, but one taste of the gray, stringy meat full of gristle was enough. He poured water for both of us from a bottle that had been in the chest, and drank his quickly. I put mine carefully aside after noticing specks of dust floating in it.

"What's your name, girl?" he asked after a while.

"Emily."

"Emily what?"

"Emily Adair." I thought that if he knew Pa had adopted me and given me his name Hasty would never let me go.

"Well, Emily Adair, if Simon marries you you'll be Emily Lawrence—"

"I will not marry—"

"Oh, yes you will. Simon generally gets what he wants." He paused and stared at me for a few minutes and then muttered, "But maybe he won't this time."

I kept quiet for a while and then asked if Simon was a rich man. Hasty grunted and got up to take a bottle of whiskey from the chest. He poured a generous amount into the metal cup he'd used earlier and tossed it off. Then he refilled the cup and sat down again.

"Is Simon rich, she asks! Is water wet? Yes, he's rich, an' he wants to be richer, rich enough to 'stablish himself in a fine place like his brother did. Almost ready to, I'd say, and now that John's out of the way he won't be stuck out there on that island no more."

He poured a third drink of whiskey, and after seating himself on the edge of the bunk, turned to face me. When he began to speak again, a faraway look came into his eyes and his tone became almost confidential.

"Ah, yes, Simon's comin' into his own now. I allus thought someday he'd kick over the traces, and one day he did."

He paused, setting the cup carefully on one of the stools. The dreamy look in his eyes was replaced by a sudden gleam, as if he had just realized what Simon's wealth might mean to him. While I waited for him to continue I noted that for all his coarse behavior and rough speech he was not an ill-favored man. Before I knew it I was making a study of his face, just as I had made of Simon's before I started my first sketch of him.

What I could see of Jack Hasty's hair under the ever-present top hat was dark brown, almost black, and curled slightly behind ears that grew close to his head. His features were well disposed, quite regular, in fact, the eyes slightly shifty but an attractive greenish-brown, the nose aquiline, and the mouth well formed. It was, with the exception of the deep lines that ran from each side of his nose almost to his chin, the face of a young man, but I guessed him to be about Pa's age, which would put him in his mid-forties.

He was bigger than either Pa or Simon, well set up, with broad shoulders, narrow hips, and long legs. It occurred to me that given the right clothes and a bit of drilling in proper speech, he could easily pass for a gentleman in polite society. Whatever had led him to his manner of life? I wondered. Had he once been a child of the streets, a homeless boy who stole for his livelihood and slept in doorways like so many of the city's ragged children? If so, he had by some miracle avoided an early death from cold, hunger, or disease, so often the fate of the children of poverty and so different from the boyhoods of Pa and Simon. What, I wondered, would Jack Hasty be like if he'd been brought up by an Aunt Becky?

At the thought of Pa I sighed, causing Hasty to look at me sharply and ask what was the matter.

"You said that now that John Lawrence was gone Simon would come into his own."

"So I did," he said, nodding his head, "an' so he will, so long as he behaves himself."

"Were they not brothers and in a partnership?" I asked.

"Ay, that they were, but John held the reins, an' Simon was champin' at the bit," he said, yawning and getting to his feet.

"Why was John Lawrence killed?" I asked, thinking that by this time the whiskey might have loosened his tongue. "Did Simon do it?"

"You ask too many questions, girl," he answered with another yawn, "an' I need some sleep." With that he threw himself down on the bunk opposite the one I'd used. Moments later he began to snore.

I was lucky that Hasty hadn't asked me how I knew that Pa had been killed. That was a mistake, but perhaps the whiskey had dulled his wits, after all. There was no guarantee, though, that he wouldn't remember my question when he woke up.

I had no desire to sleep myself, and after propping myself up on the pillow I'd used earlier I waited as patiently as I could for the resumption of our voyage. Sometime later, an hour or more, I judged, the door to the cabin burst open and Doakes hopped over the raised threshold.

"Storm's over, Jack!" he shouted. "Time we was movin', eh?"

Hasty was on his feet at once, looking as refreshed and clear-eyed as a man who'd had a full night's sleep after drinking nothing stronger than lemonade. Once we were under way again I sat quietly trying to fit together the bits of information I already had with those I'd picked up since I saw the oysterman (I still didn't know the name of the boat) enter the cove at Grape Island. If I'd had access to pen and paper I'd have written them down, but as it was I could only count off the facts on my fingers—and with them, the new questions they raised.

1. Jack Hasty was a river pirate who had done business with Simon and Pa for at least eight years.
2. The boxes I had seen in Hasty's house all those years ago were similar to the ones that were unloaded at the cove. What did they contain?
3. Pa had questioned me closely about Hasty's boxes, asking if I'd opened any of them.
4. When I described Fat Sally's quarters to Pa he had not been at all surprised at the expensive and luxurious furnishings. Had Pa known her?
5. Did Hasty tell Pa he'd sent me to Fat Sally's?
6. Simon had resented Pa. Was he angry enough to have him murdered, or to do it himself? He had appeared at the house on Colonnade Row only hours after Pa's death. He could have gone to John Street

to get cleaned up and then returned.

7. Finally, how was I to get away from Hasty and Doakes, and where would I go?

It was raining lightly when we docked at the foot of Fulton Street early in the evening. Doakes tied up, and as I stepped ashore, flanked by the two men, I saw with surprise the name *Flora* painted on the bow.

"Why is she called the *Flora*?" I asked.

"Simon's doin'," Hasty answered with a shrug. "Used to be the *E. A. Taplow*, but he had 'er rechristened after John died."

Out in the open on South Street, where all manner of cargo was being moved on and off the tall-masted, ocean-going vessels, I felt more at home than I'd ever felt on Grape Island, and some instinct told me that I would never have a better chance of eluding my captors than here in the noise and confusion of the waterfront.

"First a meal," Hasty said, leading us toward an eating place across from the docks. "Then you go back to the *Flora* for the night, Doakes. Nothin' to steal on her now, but some of them fellers from the Border gang or the Swamp Angels might smash up the cabin just for the hell of it."

"Where're you takin' the girl, Jack?" Doakes asked. "An' when'll you be back?"

"Never mind about her, Doakes. I'll see you sometime tomorrer."

Nothing more was said until we'd found a table in a small, noisy restaurant noted, a sign said, for its fish chowder. The food was indeed good, and in spite of lack of sleep and the discomfort of the cabin on the *Flora* I began to feel the strength returning to my body. Hasty sent Doakes back to the boat after the stocky seaman had had a single tankard of ale with his meal, and then he ordered a second one for himself. He drank it slowly, frowning slightly and casting occasional glances at me.

"We'll go to my place for the night," he said at last, "an' see how things go. All the comforts a girl could want, see?"

"I don't want to go to your place," I said as firmly as I could. "I have friends—"

"Too bad," he retorted. "You're comin' to my place to be my woman. I like you, girl."

"What will your wife say?" I asked, remembering the woman named Mag.

"Long dead," he replied. "Cholera got her. Now what do you say?"

"No, no, absolutely no!"

A little smile played around his mouth, but he said nothing and continued to drink his ale. I didn't know what to do except look for a chance to get away. As I waited I watched people

179

crowding around the bar and then shifted my attention to those at the tables, most of whom had large bowls of chowder in front of them.

One woman in particular caught my eye. She wore a low-cut, bright red dress of some shiny material decorated with tiny gold and silver bells at the bodice that tinkled as she moved rather tipsily among the tables, laughing and joking with their occupants. Hasty's frown deepened when he saw her coming toward us, and suddenly he said that it was time to leave. But it was too late. The woman had already spotted him, and before he could stand up she was leaning across the table patting his face with heavily ringed fingers.

"Jack!" she exclaimed, "yer back! Where've ya been, darlin' boy?"

Without waiting for an answer she pulled the table out, planted herself on his lap, and twining her arms around his neck began to kiss him passionately on the mouth. I didn't wait to see what happened next. I pushed my chair back as far as it would go, crouched down, and made for the door.

Moments later I was out on South Street with the sounds of derisive laughter and cat-calls ringing in my ears. I ran as fast as I could through the rain, which by that time had turned into a downpour, but I had barely reached the corner when Hasty caught up with me. Without a word he picked me up and carried me, screaming and protesting, through a series of narrow streets and alleys. No one paid any attention to my cries for help. Maybe there were no people about—I couldn't see very well with my head pressed against Hasty's broad shoulder.

Suddenly Hasty tripped, stumbled, or slipped over something, and we both sprawled on the wet pavement. I heard him groan and saw him reach out to grab hold of me before I backed away and ran off through the rain. I wasn't hurt in the fall and hurried along blindly, not caring where I was going as long as I put distance between me and Jack Hasty. But once I saw the bulk of Trinity Church rising up in front of me I knew where I was—not far at all from 42 Church Street. A short time later a startled Madame Fortier found me slumped against her front door and half led, half carried me into the warmth of her little house.

❧ · *Chapter XVI* · ❧

"NO, NO, *ma petite!* You must not dream of leaving your bed until you are rid of that wretched cold," Madame admonished me sternly the next morning when I started to get up. "And for a while you must not talk. Your voice is too hoarse. Here, drink this potion Jeanette has mixed for you, tea with lemon and honey. It will soothe your throat, and you will feel better. There is plenty of time for a full recital of the events that brought you here. In the meantime, be assured that Jeanette and I will keep you safe and make you well again. You were wet through last night and have caught quite a chill."

The following day my voice was better, but since Madame would not hear of my getting out of bed I was forced to lie quietly, clad in one of her embroidered nightgowns, and submit to the ministrations of the two women.

"Be patient, *chérie*," she said coaxingly, "and this *aprés-midi* Jeanette and I will bring our *chocolat* up here and you shall tell us all that has happened."

What with all their comments and interruptions it took longer than the hours that afternoon afforded to tell them the whole story. Because of their many questions I had to go back and describe what life was like in Colonnade Row after Madame's departure. I tried to be fair to Pa, but when I told about the renovation of Madame's room, about his reaction to Hugh Carberry, and about how his attitude toward me had changed, they both looked shocked.

"He was gradually limiting my activities, Madame," I said, remembering how he had put an end to the art school lessons, "and as time went on . . ."

"He wanted you for himself, Emily," Madame said with a sigh. "Did he propose marriage to you, *chérie?*"

"No, but he was becoming more and more free with his caresses, and they were not fatherly at all."

"Just as I thought," she said, glancing over at her sister, who looked up from her sewing and nodded in agreement. "Now it is indeed clear to me," she continued after a momentary pause, "and I shall tell you what I think. As you know, *ma petite,* you bear a striking resemblance not only to poor little Ellie, but also to her mother, Flora, or at least to the way Flora looked before she became ill. I remember well how lovely she was before the accident, her lustrous hair, her beautiful complexion, and that graceful carriage. Oh, she was a true beauty in her day! Both Mr. John Lawrence and his brother, Mr. Simon, were madly in love with her.

"Some of this I learned from Nellie—remember her? She had been Flora's maid before the marriage, and then she became housekeeper. Frequently she would spend an evening with me after Ellie was in bed for the night. It was from Nellie I heard how the brothers had struggled bitterly for Flora's hand, more than once coming to blows over her. According to Nellie, Miss Flora chose Mr. John not because of his looks—he and Mr. Simon were equally handsome—but because he was already established in the city. He could give her the life she wanted, while Mr. Simon continued to stay in the country.

"Nellie didn't know, and I never could understand, why Mr. John had the upper hand in that business in which they called themselves partners. That is something of a mystery. Certainly they were not equal partners. In any case, Mr. Simon remained out on that island and seldom

185

came to the house. I think he married—"

"Yes, he did, Madame," I interrupted. "But it was not a happy marriage. His wife ran off, leaving him with an infant boy, Paul. She drowned later on. But tell me, Madame, do you know anything about the business the two brothers were engaged in?"

"Oh, yes," she answered quickly. "It was an importing firm. The office is, or was, on John Street. I remember how Mr. John would joke about being on a street named for him. Then, of course, he did business at home. Those men who came at night were agents he employed, men who were free only in the evening. I suppose their daytime hours were employed in the collecting or selling of the imported goods."

How right you are, I thought, and after the goods were collected (or, more accurately, stolen) and sold, the proceeds were brought to Pa under cover of the night, at least the ones that were not shipped out to Grape Island.

"And," Madame went on, "you say that Mr. Simon came the day you found poor Mr. John dead and took you and Anna out to the island? Why did he not wait until after the funeral?"

"He said the funeral would be on Grape Island and that we had to go at once. I don't know why. Then he told me that he'd promised Pa to see to my safety. As for Anna, she had no place to go—the other servants had disappeared—and she was frightened, so when she said she could cook and clean, Simon decided to take her along. I was glad to have her with me, too."

I sighed and lay back against the pillows, causing Madame to say we'd done enough talking for one day and that tomorrow she would see about some clothing for me.

"What you were wearing is beyond repair, Emily, and not fit for a gentlewoman. In the morning I shall go out early and find something suitable, and then we shall see what else is needed. Rest now for an hour, *ma petite*, and then you may put on this robe and come downstairs for a light supper with Jeanette and me."

She neatly folded the soft woolen robe, placed it at the foot of the bed, and kissed me lightly on the forehead, just as she had so many times in the past.

"And tomorrow," she said, pausing with her hand on the doorknob, "you will tell us how you came to be wandering about the city in such a terrible downpour, and with no cloak, no protection against the rain."

༃

"Now that you have so nicely recovered,

Emily," Madame said one morning almost a week after my arrival at her house, "do you not think it would be wise to write to Mr. Simon, to let him know that you are safe? He apparently honored his brother's request to take care of you, and I would think he would be quite worried about your safety after your sudden disappearance. He will probably be quite angry with that Mr. Jack Hasty."

"Yes, I suppose I should," I answered absently. "I shall write at once, Madame." That I was feeling despondent that morning had nothing to do with Simon or my recent illness and everything to do with a notice I had seen in the society news in the newspaper, an announcement of the engagement of Mr. Hugh Carberry to Lady Enid Grenville of Bellingham Court, Sussex, England. How could he? He had said he loved me, asked me to wait for him. . . . No wonder both he and Carrie had stopped writing to me.

"Yes, Madame," I said, bringing my thoughts back to the present. "He will be concerned, and so will Anna—poor Anna, always working so hard. Yes, I shall write at once. Also, Madame, I cannot go on being dependent on you and Jeanette. No, no, do not protest, just listen to me. I think Pa, Mr. John Lawrence, might have made some provision for me one way or another, although Simon said he inherited everything. And even if he didn't name me in his will, wouldn't I, as his adopted daughter, have some right to an inheritance? Perhaps I should consult a lawyer."

"Just write to Simon, *chérie*," Madame said. "See what he says before you take any steps."

> 42 Church Street
> New York
> April 15, 1859

Dear Simon,

I had no intention of leaving Grape Island the night you returned from the city. Jack Hasty and a man named Doakes forced me onto the *Flora* and brought me to New York. I escaped from them and have been staying with Madame Fortier, who was my governess when I lived in Colonnade Row. I would like to see you, Simon, to talk over some matters of importance.

Please give Anna and Paul my love and tell them that I miss them.

> Sincerely yours,
> Emily

P.S. Jack Hasty said he would make you pay handsomely for my return, but he doesn't know where I am now.

Grape Island
April 20, 1859

Dear Emily,

I am glad that you are in safe hands. With your permission I will call on you on Saturday, April 24, at 10 o'clock in the morning.

Sincerely,
Simon

"What exactly did Hasty say to you, Emily?" Simon asked after Madame had shown him into the little French parlor and left us alone.

"Just that you owed him something and would have to pay dearly if you wanted me back. But Simon—"

"Did he say how much?" Simon interrupted.

"No, but from the way he spoke I gathered that it would be a substantial sum."

"I see," he said, drawing a long breath. "How did he get hold of you, anyway? Were you down at the cove that night?"

"Yes," I answered slowly, "I was. Before she died, Aunt Becky warned me that Grape Island was no place for me and urged me to leave before it was too late. She didn't have either the time or the strength to say more. I was worried, but when Billy told me you would be coming

190

back on the boat with a shipment, I was more curious than frightened."

"So you watched us unload the boat?"

"Yes, and after you left in the wagon with Billy and Josh I started to follow you, but I slipped and rolled down a slope. Jack Hasty almost stepped on me."

"Were you hurt?" he asked anxiously, genuine concern showing in his dark eyes.

"Just bruised a little," I answered and went on to describe the trip in the *Flora* without going into too much detail. I had just finished telling him how I managed to elude Hasty, when Jeanette knocked on the door and came in with a tray of coffee and little cakes. She smiled shyly when Simon stood up to hold the door for her and then left the room in a flurry of silk and lace. She had changed from her usual plain morning dress to something she thought appropriate for our visitor. I think she was impressed by his good looks and a little embarrassed to be caught staring at him. He did present a handsome appearance that morning in a new pale yellow waistcoat, a freshly laundered white cravat, and a well-fitted tan jacket with braided cuffs. He had had his hair carefully trimmed, making his resemblance to Pa even more striking than usual.

"Simon," I said after we'd taken a few sips of

coffee, "there's something on my mind. I've been meaning to ask you—"

"About money?" he asked with a smile.

"No, no. Not that. Pa told you about my childhood experience with Jack Hasty, didn't he? How he locked me in a room in his house and then sold me to Fat Sally?"

"Yes, he did, Emily," he answered, nodding his head. "But what has that to do with me?"

"Maybe nothing, Simon. But what I cannot understand is why you and Pa would have anything to do with a criminal like Hasty. Apparently he's been bringing those so-called shipments out to the island for years. Why are you involved with such a dangerous man? Aren't you afraid of him? Before I ran away from him he said he wanted me to be his 'woman.' "

"Of all the—oh, my dear, I—how dare he! I'll—"

He didn't say what he would do but sat back in the tapestried chair and fixed his eyes on me before speaking again.

"Hasty is a problem, Emily, a nasty problem, and has been for years, first for John and then for me. He won't be easy to deal with, but I shall try. In fact, I am doing all I can to disassociate myself from him. I never wanted to have anything to do with him in the first place, but John, well, he couldn't help himself. I'll tell you someday how that came about. In the meantime you seem to be safe enough here. Hasty never knew anything about Madame Fortier, did he?"

"No, I don't think so."

"That's good. Now, I've been thinking over your request for funds. I told you that John did not leave you anything, and that's the truth, but I do feel that he intended to do so. He would not have left you penniless, so I shall see that you have an income of your own."

He took a leather purse from one of his pockets and placed it carefully on the marqueterie table. "This should be enough for your immediate needs, Emily, and after I straighten out a few business matters we'll make arrangements for something permanent."

I thanked him and was about to ask him why he had suddenly changed his mind when he stood up, saying he must leave.

"Before I go, let me say, Emily, that I apologize, sincerely and abjectly, for the abrupt way I refused your request when you made it out on the island. All I can say on my behalf is that I was not myself that morning and that I do regret—"

"Simon, it's all right. I know that you have grave matters on your mind and that you had never bargained to have me on your hands."

"No," he said with a slight smile, "I never

did, but neither have I ever regretted that you came into my life. Now, I really must go. Stay here, Emily, until you hear from me, and if you go out make sure one of these charming French women is with you. Don't go alone."

❧

I had great difficulty persuading Madame to accept any payment for my board and for the clothes she had purchased for me, and it was not until I said that I couldn't bear to feel like a burden that she agreed to take what I offered.

"You could never, never be a burden, *ma petite*," she said, shaking her head. "You are the daughter I never had, you see. But we cannot have you feeling like a charity case. I shall put this aside for the present, and maybe someday Jeanette and I will find a special use for it. Now, shall we go to the little dressmaker on Hudson Street and see about another spring costume for you? Have you enough money left for that?"

I assured her that Simon had been generous, that I had plenty, and let her persuade me to order not one but two complete outfits for which Jeanette would make suitable hats. I also bought painting materials, canvases, and sketching pads, and coaxed both my landladies into sitting for their portraits. I hoped that if I

194

kept busy I would be able to put all thoughts of Hugh Carberry out of my mind.

Keeping occupied did help, but only up to a point. I seldom fell asleep immediately upon going to bed, and during the hour or so before I closed my eyes for the night I could not help remembering how he had looked at me, how he had held me in his arms, and how first the tenderness and then the ardor of his kisses had inflamed my body. Then the tears would begin to flow and keep on flowing until I fell asleep, exhausted and unhappy.

❧· *Chapter XVII* ·❧

J EANETTE WANTED TO be painted wearing her best hat, and I was having trouble with the soft feathers that nestled close to her fading blond hair. Feathers and hair were almost the same color, and I was afraid she'd look as if she had a head full of the former by the time the portrait was finished. I was about to ask her if she hadn't another favorite hat when the message from Simon came, putting an end to the sitting.

"For you, Emily," Madame said, bustling into the room and handing me a rather soiled envelope. "Such a rude young man brought it! Such dirty hands! And he demanded ten cents before he would give it to me—said the gentleman told him to hurry and that he'd run all the way. Why, *chérie*, you look so anxious. What is it?"

I handed her the note I'd taken from the envelope, and she read it aloud: " 'Emily, come as soon as you can to the Tombs and ask to see the warden. Urgent! Simon.' "

۞

The sign on the door of the room to which Madame and I were directed said WARDEN in letters large enough to be commensurate with the size of the man who rose from behind the most enormous desk I had ever seen. "I am John W. Powell," he announced in a gravelly voice, "the warden of this house of detention. You must be Miss Emily Lawrence, and you, missus, are?"

"I am Madame Jacque Fortier, chaperone to Miss Lawrence," Madame answered quietly.

"I see, missus," he said, looking her over suspiciously, as if she might be concealing a dangerous weapon. "Well, you wait right here and have a seat, missus, while I take the young lady to the prisoner's cell, and don't try to go no place. A guard will be at the door."

"I have no intention of leaving," Madame said frostily. "Take your time, Emily, and see how you can help Simon."

"He'll need more help than she can give him, missus," the warden muttered, motioning me toward the door. "Watch your step, miss. There's holes in this fine carpet, been there for years."

We went down a short hall at the end of which two guards were slouching against the wall. "Stand up straight, you lazy buggers," the warden shouted, "and Bummer, you get yourself down to my office and don't let anyone in or out until I come back. Get goin'! Rafe, you foller me!"

He unlocked a large metal door and I followed him into a passageway lined on either side with noisy, iron-barred cells. My heart sank when I saw the occupants: some were chained to the floor, others were sitting disconsolately on cots with one hand shackled to the wall. I heard obscenities shouted at the guard, and catcalls, which I supposed were meant for me. I felt slightly sick at the thought of Simon's being somewhere in their midst, but I breathed more easily when we passed out of the noisome room and climbed a narrow flight of stairs to the floor above.

"This way, miss," the warden said, turning to the right. "Your man's down this way."

It was quiet on the upper floor, not a peaceful quiet, I thought, but the quiet that accompanies despair. I saw Simon before the warden unlocked the door to his cell and was surprised at the surge of emotion that swept through me at the sight of him standing at the high, small window with his elbow on the stone sill, just as I had seen him stand so many times at the fireplace in the warm, friendly kitchen on Grape Island.

He smiled when he saw me and started to speak, only to be interrupted by the warden's rasping voice. "Fifteen minutes, miss. That's all that's allowed. Rafe here will tell you when the time is up and bring you back to my office. Don't try anything, Mr. Lawrence." With that he locked the cell door once more and left.

Simon took my arm and guided me over to where he'd been standing under the window, as far away from the guard as possible.

"Oh, Simon—"

"It's all right, Emily. Don't be upset. As you can see, I'm in one of the luxury cells, one of those reserved for people who can pay. See, it's complete with bed, washstand, table, and chair."

"But Simon, why—"

"It's all Hasty's doing. He managed to get me arrested on false evidence. It's too long a story to tell in fifteen minutes. It'll have to wait."

"How can I help? What—"

"There are two things you can do for me. First, you've seen him, Hasty, I mean, close up, haven't you?"

"Oh, yes, too close."

"All right. Not too many people have. He's kept undercover for years, so very few know what he looks like. John did, and I do, but the man's a wizard at avoiding the police. He wasn't the one to be there when they arrested me; he gave the orders and his henchmen carried them out. You saw him at work on the *Flora*, though; that's the real Hasty. I saw him that night, too. Remember, I traveled out on the boat with him. That's the original Jack Hasty, top hat and all."

"Do you know why he wears that hat, Simon?"

"I've no idea. Maybe he's bald on top. But listen to me, Emily. We haven't much time. The police want him, but they have no clear idea what he looks like. Could you—I mean, you're good at sketching faces, Aunt Becky's and mine—could you make a sketch of Hasty's? It would be helpful, really, Emily."

"I might be able to do it, Simon," I said hesitantly, trying to remember the details of the face I had studied that night on the *Flora*. "I've always worked from a model, though, and it might not be accurate."

"It will be better than nothing, believe me. See how quickly you can do it, and bring it here to me. As soon as Hasty is caught I'll be out of here."

"Time's up," the guard called through the bars. "Time to go, miss."

"Emily, you didn't come alone, did you?"

Simon asked, catching hold of my hand as the door to the cell swung open.

"No, no, Madame is waiting in the warden's office."

"Come along, miss," the guard said, rattling his keys.

"I'm coming, I'm coming," I cried, pulling my hand away from Simon's warm grasp and trying to smile at him encouragingly. "I'll bring it tomorrow, Simon."

He led me slowly over to the door, and then as I looked back at him through the bars he murmured softly, "No wonder John loved you so much, Emily."

As Madame and I walked briskly back to Church Street I described the interview with Simon in detail, all but his final remark, and said I would have to start work on the sketch at once.

"Of course you must, *chérie*," she said emphatically, nodding her head so vigorously that the artificial flowers on the brim of her hat trembled. "I will see that you are not disturbed, and when you are ready I shall go back with you to that dreadful place to deliver the sketch to Mr. Simon."

છે

Producing a lifelike sketch from memory

seemed at first to be an impossible task, but after a few false starts a fairly good resemblance to Jack Hasty began to emerge. In the end I drew two views, one in profile and the other full face. I wasn't completely satisfied with either of them, but I thought they might do for purposes of identification. It was almost midnight when I put my pencil down and prepared to go to bed, and I had a nagging feeling that I had forgotten something. Just before I fell asleep I knew what it was: I had not asked Simon about his second request.

The next morning I took the precaution of folding the sketches carefully into one of the pockets of my patterned challis skirt before we set out for the Tombs. Madame, who of course had never seen Jack Hasty, commented that in my drawings he looked like a pirate in a top hat. Yes, I said to myself, you are correct, Madame. He is a pirate, or perhaps the king of the river pirates, and the top hat is in lieu of a crown. I said nothing, however; she was already nervous enough.

⁂

"I have brought Mr. Lawrence some fruit, Mr. Powell," I said, holding out the small basket Jeanette had packed for the warden's inspection. "May I give it to him?"

He dumped the oranges, apples, and pears out onto his desk and after examining the empty basket allowed me to replace the fruit. I saw Madame's lips twitch and knew what she was thinking: just before we left the house she, Jeanette, and I had discussed secreting the sketches underneath the fruit. Only at the last minute had we decided against it.

This time the warden didn't bother to escort me upstairs but sent Rafe instead. The guard was a talkative fellow, and after we'd discussed the weather I asked him if his real name was Ralph. He said no, that his mother had a picture she liked of the Virgin and child painted by some foreigner named Raphael, so that was what she called her firstborn son.

"The pitcher hangs over her bed," he said. "Can't say I think much of it, a sad-lookin' dame holdin' a fat kid who looks like he has a bellyache. An' I never liked my name, neither, but I guess I'm stuck with it. Here we are, miss. Fifteen minutes is all. I'll be right at the end of this here hall. There's a ledge there where I can sit and rest these achin' legs—too much standin'."

❧

The anxious look I saw on Simon's face when I

entered the cell changed to one of satisfaction as he unfolded the sketches and spread them on the small table.

"You've caught him, Emily," he said softly, "shifty eyes and all. The full face is better than the profile, but they'll both be helpful. I'm grateful to you."

"Do you want me to give them to the police?" I asked after a moment or two while he continued to study the sketches.

"No, no. I'll take care of that. I've a fellow, Jim Wells, working for me. He's not really a detective, but he does some of that kind of thing, and he knows which people on the police force to go to, the ones who are interested in, and I might say baffled by, Jack Hasty."

"Simon, I still don't know what you are doing here in the Tombs," I said as I watched him refold the sketches. "Can't you tell me now what is going on?"

"I can tell you some of it, but not all, at least not now. You see, as you said when I called on you, Hasty wanted a large sum to turn you over to me, a hundred thousand dollars—yes, a hundred thousand! He came by my office on John Street looking to collect it, insisting that it was due him even though you'd escaped from him. He said that given time (he'd been busy with other things) he'd find you and bring you to me, but he wanted the money in advance. Sometimes I think he's crazy, but if he's a lunatic, he's a damn clever one.

"Anyway, when I refused to give him even a partial payment he was livid and said I'd regret it. Then he had the office watched, and when I left there—that was a couple of days after I'd been to see you—two of his men set upon me and created a scene in the street. One of them held me while the other one planted a gold watch and chain in my pocket, and when the police arrived I was accused of theft and arrested.

"My lawyer, a good man, says he'll have me out of here in a week or ten days, and he will. Of that I am sure. I'll turn these sketches over to him when he comes in later today, and then he and Jim Wells will work with the police in their search for Hasty. He's wanted for almost every crime on the books."

"I cannot understand it," I said, thinking back to my introduction to Jack Hasty after John Ireland's death. "Lunatic or not, he must be either brilliant or extremely lucky to have avoided the police for so long. Tell me, Simon, how did you and Pa come to be associated with him?"

"I cannot go into that now, Emily. It's too complicated, and there isn't time. I will explain it all to you later. In the meantime, there is something else I'd like you to do for me: I'm concerned about Paul. He had a cold when I left. Dr. Simpkins said he'd keep an eye on him, but I haven't heard from him. I know this is asking a lot of you, but—well, Anna does the best she can—but could you, would you go out to Grape Island and take charge of things until I can get there?"

He paused, and when I did not respond immediately he went on. "I know you want to study painting here in New York, and I also know I'm imposing on your good nature, but it wouldn't be for long, Emily, and it would set my mind at rest about Paul. He's so vulnerable."

His concern for Paul was clearly evident not only in the catch in his voice when he mentioned his son's name but also in the anxious expression with which he regarded me. He kept his eyes on my face for a moment, then turned away, moving over to stand under the small, dusty window.

He didn't coax me, he didn't plead with me to go; that would not have been in keeping with Simon's character. He simply made his request and waited.

"Fifteen minutes, miss," Rafe called as he approached the cell rattling his keys. "You'll have to leave now."

"Of course I'll do it, Simon," I heard myself saying. "I'll come see you tomorrow morning before I take the train in case you have any messages for Josh and Billy."

He strode across the short distance between us and took me in his arms, murmuring, "Bless you, Emily." Then he stood back and, smiling down at me, said quietly, "And *you* will be safer there, my dear, out of Hasty's reach."

⸙

Madame Fortier and Jeanette were predictably upset when I told them of my plans, and only after extracting a promise that I would return to them as soon as possible did they agree that I was doing the right thing. They insisted on accompanying me not only to the prison, where Simon gave me a list of things to be done on the island, but also to the railroad station across the river. They waited on the platform until the train pulled out, and when I waved to them from the window I could see that both women were close to tears. Madame, however, managed a little smile, along with so many encouraging nods that the silk flowers on her hat threatened to break loose and whirl away in the breeze.

♋· *Chapter XVIII* ·♋

THE SUN WAS setting when I reached the little station in Mattituck, and by the time I made my way to the dock and found a fisherman to ferry me across to Grape Island, dusk had fallen. It was barely light enough for me to see the narrow path on which Anna and I had slipped and slid last winter, and I sighed with relief when I heard Shamrock barking and saw the light that streamed out from the kitchen.

No one could have asked for a warmer welcome than the one I received that night. Anna burst out crying as she hugged me, young Paul danced around clamoring for my attention, Josh pulled a chair for me, and Billy helped me off with my jacket.

"Oh, Miss Emily, Miss Emily!" Anna wailed. "We was so worrit about you! Where in the world did you go? The bed empty—oh, miss! Oh, the corn bread. Josh, take it outta the oven. An' where's Mr. Simon?"

"Soup's hot, Anna," Josh called. "Set a place for Miss Emily, willya? Likely she's hungry."

Anna reluctantly let go of me, and a few minutes later the five of us sat down to a supper of chicken soup, hot corn bread, stewed apples, and cookies. By the time Josh poured the coffee I had assured them that Simon was safe in New York (I didn't mention the Tombs) and had answered their questions about my abrupt departure from the island. I could see that they were shocked that I should take it upon myself to spy on Simon, but I made no excuses for my actions beyond saying that Aunt Becky had warned me that something evil was going on.

"Somehow I do not think all this was Simon's fault," I said slowly, looking from one serious face to another. "I think Jack Hasty is behind everything. Speaking of Hasty, if he shows up here, and he may, if he eludes the police, do not allow him into the house. We'll keep the doors and windows locked, and also, no one is to go any distance away alone, always with someone else. Paul, do you understand me?"

"An' what's this Hasty person look like, miss?" Anna asked. " 'Ow will I know 'im?"

"I made a sketch of him while I was on the train," I answered. "Paul, would you hand me my bag, please? It's over there on that chair."

"That's him, all right," Billy said as the rough sketch was passed around the table. "Ain't it, Josh?"

"Sure is," Josh nodded. "Hat an' all."

"Of course, he may not bother us," I said, suddenly remembering what Simon had said about my being safe on Grape Island, "but he's a greedy man and might want to get hold of the boxes he helped unload from the boat. You see, he and Simon have had a disagreement. What happened to those boxes, anyway? What did Simon do with them? Are they in the barn?"

"No, miss," Josh looked puzzled as he replied. "Nothin' in the barn but what's s'posed to be there. Used to be some boxes there, but the morning after we unloaded the boat—even before we knowed you was gone—Mr. Simon took everything over to the mainland. We hadda make three trips in the wherry. I don't know what happened to all the stuff after that, but Mr. Simon was gone all day, and when he came back, just after dark it was, and found you wasn't here he near had a fit. Remember, Bill?"

"Won't be nothin' there for Hasty if he does come," Billy said, nodding his head. "An' if he comes he better watch out—he shouldna taken you off like that, miss."

"Well," I said, glancing at each concerned

211

face in turn, "as I said, he may not come here, but in the meantime, while we're waiting for Simon to get back, will you, Billy, make sure all the doors and downstairs windows are locked? And Josh, if Paul is out in the barn with you, keep him right by your side, will you?"

They both nodded, looking as serious and self-important as if I had charged them with the protection of the realm and all of its inhabitants.

"That was a delicious supper, Anna," I said, rising and pushing my chair back, "but now I must get some sleep. Come on, Paul, it's time you went to bed, too. How is your cold, by the way?"

"All gone, Em'ly. Wasn't bad. The worst thing was the cough medicine Doc Simpkins made me take. Ugh! How about tellin' me a story after I'm in bed, Em'ly?"

🙶

"Makes me and Josh wash our own clothes, she does," Billy grumbled at the breakfast table the next day.

"Yeah, bosses us around all right," Josh agreed with a little smile at Anna. "But she feeds us good. Did you say Mr. Simon gave you a list, miss?"

When I handed him the slip of paper Simon had given me, he glanced at it briefly and handed it back. "You better read it out, miss. His writin's not that good."

A little while later he and Billy were out in the warm spring sun turning over the vegetable patch, and as Anna and I sat over a last cup of coffee we could hear them talking to Paul, shooing Shamrock out of the way, and arguing amiably about where to put the beans and when was the proper time to plant onions.

"I'm glad that you're here, miss," Anna said, smiling happily. "I can get them to do some things. . . ."

"I think you've managed very well, Anna. The house is clean."

"One room each day, miss. That's my way. Today it's the parlor, not that that is ever very bad. Tomorrer the kitchen—I could clean that every day, an' most days I do give it a lick and a promise. Once a week a good turnin' out. Them boys know better now than to come in without wipin' their feet, so it ain't so bad. An' they help with the washin' up at night. I said if they didn't they could do their own cookin', an' that scared 'em."

Simon needn't have worried, I thought. Paul's cold was cured, and Anna, like a good house-keeper, had set up a plan and was making it work.

She let me help with some of the lighter house-work, dusting, folding the laundry, and sweeping the front porch, but she was adamant in her refusal to let me scrub anything, even the old sink in the kitchen. In her book that would not be "fittin'."

I set aside an hour every morning for Paul's lessons in the fundamentals of the three Rs. On warm days we sat on the porch, and in bad weather we worked at the Pembroke table in the parlor window, but on the whole, Grape Island was lovely that spring.

It did rain occasionally, and I was sitting at the parlor window one morning, watching the water drip down from the porch roof and wondering when Simon would come back, when I realized that I was surprisingly content with the life I had been leading for the better part of a month. It took me a while to figure out why my attitude toward Grape Island had changed so completely, and then suddenly I knew: for the first time in my life I was needed. Simon needed me as his surrogate, Paul needed me to take care of him, Josh and Billy needed me as a figure of authority, someone in control, and Anna, dear Anna, simply loved me. Maybe Pa had needed me, but certainly John Ireland hadn't, Madame could easily have found another pupil, and apparently Hugh Carberry could do very well without me. I didn't want to think about him. . . .

"There, Em'ly, I finished the sums. See if I get a star today," Paul said, bringing me back to the morning's lesson. "Aren't they neat?"

"Very neat, Paul dear," I said, conscious of the earnest little face so close to mine. "And every one is correct. We'll save this page and put it with the ones to show your father."

"When's he coming, Em'ly?"

"Soon, dear. I don't know exactly when."

The day before I'd had a short note from Simon in which he told me to take what money I needed for household expenses from the strongbox on the top shelf of the closet in his office.

"The key to the box is hanging on a hook behind the framed copy of the charter to the island," he wrote. "You can write to me here at 17 John Street. I've been delayed, but it can't be helped. Yours, Simon."

I disliked the idea of touching any of his private possessions, but on Friday of that week when Anna showed me a list of supplies we needed from Mattituck I was forced to unlock the box and remove twenty dollars from it. I left a note to that effect on top of the remaining bills—I didn't count them, but I judged there to be at least two hundred dollars, maybe more—and gave the money to Anna along with a brief reply to Simon's letter for her to mail.

The day was overcast, somewhat chilly, and after she and Josh left, Paul and I sat down in front of the fire Billy had made in the kitchen before going over to the barn. We were engrossed in the story of Robinson Crusoe when Shamrock, who had been wandering restlessly around the room, suddenly put her paws up on the windowsill and began a shrill barking. I stood up and glanced out, thinking that she might have seen a rabbit in the vegetable garden, but that wasn't it.

"She wants to go out," Paul said, pushing his chair away from the table. "All right, Sham, come on!"

When he opened the door the dog dashed out, barking frantically, and a sudden gust of wind knocked over one of the oil lamps. For some reason I suddenly felt unsafe and on edge alone in that big house with little Paul, and before we sat down again I went around checking the locks on doors and windows. I tried to tell myself that the lowering clouds, the wind, and the rain were enough to make anyone feet uneasy, but that didn't help much.

The rest of the morning passed so slowly that at one point I thought the kitchen clock had stopped. When Paul said that the rain was letting up and asked if we couldn't go over to the barn and look for eggs, I jumped at the chance to leave the house and the nervous mood into which I had fallen. It was a good move; Billy's large presence was comforting, and after we had gathered six eggs he was only too happy to have help with the never-ending job of cleaning up. At a little after noon Paul said he was hungry, and as the three of us crossed the road and headed for the kitchen we saw Anna and Josh coming back from the dock with a small, frightened-looking black child walking between them.

"We had to bring her, miss," Anna said, watching my face for signs of disapproval. "She's been left behind and has no place to go."

"Of course you did," I said quickly, smiling at the rather pretty girl who clung to Anna's hand. She seemed to be about twelve or thirteen years old and looked as ill-clothed and ill-fed as the waifs I had seen at Fat Sally's. "You must be hungry," I said to her. "What is your name, and how old are you?"

"Tenth, ma'am," she answered in a surprisingly cultured voice, "and I'm sixteen."

"Tenth?" I repeated, puzzled.

"Yes, ma'am. Mama ran out of names when I came, and because I was the tenth baby she said she'd call me that until she thought of a better one. She never did, though."

"She's a runaway slave, Miss Emily," Josh

whispered as we continued on toward the kitchen. "Poor kid, she's had a hard time. When we found her she was scared stiff, because she'd seen a man in Mattituck she thought was after her—one of them bounty hunters, you know. Must have been some stranger. Likely she'll tell you about it. Here, Anna, lemme get that door open for you."

⸎

Later that day, when Tenth was washed, fed, and dressed in an assortment of Anna's and my clothes, she did tell us all her story. Her home life on a plantation in Virginia had been happy enough until the old overseer, a gruff but kindly man, had died and been replaced by a new one.

"A mean man, that Mr. Dolphus was, miss. None of us could abide him. He saw me reading a book Miss Livia up at the big house gave me—she was trying to educate me and teach me to speak right—and he tore it up and hit me with his riding crop. He beat the others, too, when he didn't think they were working hard enough."

"Didn't Miss Livia know about this?" I asked. "She sounds like a good woman."

"I don't know, miss. It wouldn't do any

good, anyway. He'd just find some other way to make us miserable. Mama told me to stay out of his way, and I tried, but he'd come after me. He wanted—"

At that point Tenth began to cry, and before I could move, Anna put her arms around her, making little soothing sounds. Josh and Billy looked embarrassed by the emotional outburst, but Paul brought tolerant smiles to their faces when he said, "Don't cry, Tenth. Em'ly'll take care of you."

When she was quiet again she went on with her story, telling us how her mother had encouraged her to run away with a group of slaves who knew about the Underground Railroad and wanted to find freedom in Canada. Everything was all right, she said, until they reached New York, where she became separated from the group.

"I went across a big river on a ferryboat, miss, because someone said we'd have to cross a river to get to Canada, and then I walked and walked and walked—I don't know how many days—until I got to where Josh and Anna found me. Is it far to Canada, miss?"

"A long way, Tenth," I answered, "and I think it would be a good idea for you to stay with us, at least for a while until you're rested up. Tell me, what did that man look like, the one you thought might be after you?"

"I was too scared to look at him for more than a minute," she said with a little shiver. "But he was big, and dressed in black, I think."

"Did he have a hat on?" I asked, wondering if Jack Hasty could be in the neighborhood.

"Show her the pitcher you drew, Miss Emily," Anna said. "See if it's him!"

"It's the same kind of hat, miss," Tenth said after studying the sketch I'd made of Hasty, "but the face—I didn't take time to see that. I just ran before he saw me. I didn't want to be caught and sent back to the plantation."

"You'll be safe here, Tenth," I said. "Would you like to stay with us for a while? And when Mr. Simon returns we'll see what's to be done."

"Oh, yes, miss, I would! And maybe he'll know how I can get to Canada," she said eagerly. "But I can't just sit here. I'll ask Anna if I can help her with something."

Whether she ever gets to Canada or not, I thought as I watched her approach Anna near the stove, Tenth will go far.

ॐ

I hoped she felt safe, for I certainly did not. I was convinced that the man she had seen was neither a bounty hunter nor one of the natives (who in

Mattituck would ever wear a top hat?) and that it had to be Hasty, who was either coming after me or planning to waylay Simon on his return. Nothing happened immediately, but the day after Tenth's arrival my fears and suspicions were heightened by what I saw from my bedroom window. I was standing quite still, looking out at nothing in particular just before dusk, when I thought I saw a dark figure step into the shelter of the hemlocks at the edge of the yard.

Perhaps there was no one there; I couldn't be sure. But no matter how many times I told myself it was all my imagination and that I had seen nothing more than an unusual juxtaposition of the hemlock branches as they moved in the evening breeze, I could not get the black-coated figure of Jack Hasty out of my mind.

I did not have a restful night.

⁂

I had further cause for alarm the next morning when Billy announced that someone had been sleeping in the shed down on our dock.

"Sure looks like someone's been sleepin' there," he repeated. "I went down to get a wrench Simon keeps there, an' I could see that the extra canvas for the wherry and the old cushion Miss Becky useta sit on had been moved. We keep them on a shelf, high up, so they don't get wet, an' they were on a bench in the corner. The canvas wasn't folded right, either, all sort of loose it was."

After telling everyone to stay close to the house, I tried to think what to do. Should I send Josh over to the mainland for help and keep Billy here for protection? No, I decided that would not be wise. Josh might run into the stranger and be forced to admit Tenth was here, and then she'd be caught and we'd all be in trouble for harboring a fugitive. In the end, feeling miserably inadequate, I did nothing. I simply waited, willing Simon to come back. I hadn't bargained for anything like this when I agreed to take charge of his household for a while.

He did come back, but not before we had another fright and Tenth had proved herself more resourceful than I would have expected. She'd taken Paul out to the far end of the vegetable garden to pull some radishes Anna wanted for lunch when it happened.

"We didn't see him, miss," she said when she'd caught her breath, "until he pushed the bushes and grapevines apart and stood looking at Paulie. He didn't pay any attention to me, and I was afraid he wanted to kidnap the boy."

"The same man you saw in Mattituck?" I asked, taking Paul up onto my lap.

"The same hat, anyway," she answered.

"An' what happened next?" Anna asked fearfully.

"He never said a word, but when he started to come closer to us, still looking at Paul, I yelled, 'Watch out! There's a snake's nest where you're stepping!' And when he looked down I grabbed Paulie and ran."

Thoroughly alarmed, I made everyone stay in the house for the rest of the day. Billy and Josh went over to the barn to milk the cow and tend to the animals, but they were quick about it, and when Simon banged on the door at suppertime we looked out the window to make sure it was he before we let him in.

☙ · *Chapter XIX* · ❧

"I T HAS TO be Hasty," Simon said when we finished telling him what had happened. "He must have escaped from jail and decided to come after me again, maybe get at me through Paul. Wants the money he says I owe him."

"Can't you notify the Mattituck police and have him arrested again, Simon?" I asked.

"I can try, Emily," he answered slowly. "But Hasty's too slippery a character to be easily caught. Let me think about it tonight, and then in the morning I'll go over and see what can be done. We can't have him hanging around here, that's for sure."

❧

He did not seem hopeful about the success of his mission when he left the next day, and I was surprised when he returned after a few hours looking cheerful, almost ebullient.

"Good news all around!" he said happily. "Hasty—of course it was he, although he gave his name as John Hogan—is gone. He was arrested last night trying to break into Will Price's barn. He wanted a place to sleep—apparently the widow turned him away from her boardinghouse. Didn't like the look of him, she said. The police believed me—they've known me for years—when I told them who he was and that he'd escaped from a New York jail. So now he's on the train to the city, under guard. I waited until the train pulled out, to be sure he stayed on it."

"So he's gone, is he, Mr. Simon?" Tenth asked.

"Gone for good," Simon nodded, "and they'll make sure he doesn't escape a second time. We can all relax now. Oh, and thank you, Tenth, for taking care of Paul. God! When I think of what might have happened to him if you hadn't been there!"

He hugged the child to him for a moment and then stood up. "All right, boys! Time to get to work. I noticed one of the rails on the pasture fence is down."

࿐

"I must talk to you, Emily," Simon said as we

sat in the old wicker chairs on the front porch after supper that night, watching the sunset and keeping an eye on Paul, who was pitching horseshoes with Josh next to the barn.

"About Tenth?" I asked, glancing at him and thinking how well he looked in spite of his prison experience. "She's a big help—"

"No, no, she's fine, a nice girl. Let her stay as long as she wants. No, it isn't Tenth, Emily, it's you I—"

"What do you mean?"

"What is it you would really like to do? Would you like to go back to your governess and her sister? Or strike out on your own?"

"I'm not sure," I answered, surprised to realize that I hadn't thought about New York in weeks.

"Well, then, I have a suggestion. See what you think of this: for years now I've been thinking of having a house of my own in the city, and now that John is gone I can afford it. He was always dead set against it. I could buy a splendid one—I never liked the one on Colonnade Row, and besides it was his, I'd never feel it was mine. Yes, I could buy a great one, and we could move in there for the winter months, spend the summers here—have the best of both places. I'd leave Billy and Josh here, Tenth and Anna if they wanted to stay, and you, Paul, and I would live in town in a fully staffed household. You'd be free to do whatever studying and painting you liked. How does that strike you?"

"It sounds wonderful," I said as he stood up to lean against the porch railing, still keeping his eyes on me so intently that I felt uncomfortable. Then shouts from Paul to come and watch him pitch horseshoes distracted us both.

"Just a minute, son," Simon called. "I'll be right there. Look, Emily, you must take your time and think things over. And there's still much you should know about the past. Come into the office in the morning; we won't be disturbed there. Yes, Paul, I'm coming."

⚄

"Do we hafta do lessons today, Em'ly?" Paul asked hopefully the next morning. "It's Saturday."

"No, no lessons today, son," Simon answered for me. "I need to go over some things with Emily. Why don't you see what Anna needs from the garden? Maybe Tenth will help you pick some wild grapes for jam. Tenth, don't look so worried. You are welcome here, understand?"

"Thank you, Mr. Simon," Tenth said, her face brightening. "I still don't know where Canada is."

228

"Somewhere along the line, Emily," Simon began once we were seated in his light, pleasant office, "you must have realized that my brother John was not the most stable person. Below that handsome, affable exterior lay a shrewd, calculating mind, and sometimes, when he didn't get his own way, it was apt to miscalculate drastically. I could give you any number of examples, but here is one that stands out: all the trouble with Hasty reverts back to John.

"My father had tied up our inheritances until we reached the age of thirty, which he claimed was the age of reason. Oh, the trustees were instructed to give us a living allowance, see that we were educated, and so on, and of course we had this property, but the big money wouldn't come until we were thirty years old. John couldn't wait. As soon as we were twenty-five he began to scheme. He wanted to marry Flora, and she wanted wealth, so he started looking around for a way to make money. He'd always liked fine furnishings, splendid old pieces like those you had in Colonnade Row, good French and English china, Oriental rugs, oaken chests. You remember some of them, don't you?"

I nodded, glancing at the handsome brass lion-headed bookends that stood on the back of Simon's desk and thinking of the Venetian mirrors and the antique silver candelabra in the dining room where Pa and I had sat night after night.

"Well," Simon continued, "he started out in a small way. He rented the house on John Street, the one he later bought, used the first floor for his office and showroom, and lived in the rooms up above. It wasn't long before he began to show a profit, not much, but some, and he was encouraged to continue. But it wasn't enough to give Flora all she wanted.

"Oh, Flora! Her grace and beauty! I was madly in love with her myself. I was no competition for John, though. He promised her the world, and all I could offer her was this, life here on Grape Island."

"Why didn't you go into business yourself, Simon?" I asked when he paused and stared out the window as if conjuring up Flora's image among the daisies and buttercups that grew wild all over the island.

"For two reasons," he answered after a moment or two. "First, my father's will stipulated that one of us was to live here, run the place, and take care of Aunt Becky, and second, I hadn't an idea in the world what I *could* do. And, of course, there was no arguing with John. So he went off, and I stayed.

"But to get back to John's business. His progress was steady, but it was slow, and he was afraid Flora wouldn't wait for him. I could see that he was nervous when he came out to see her in the summer—her family had a big estate over in Greenport, their summer home. They lived in New York in the winter.

"Yes, John was in a hurry to get rich, and one day when a fellow came in with a rare Italian casket, Florentine work—a lady's jewelry box, really—wanting to sell it, John recognized its value. He suspected it had been stolen, but he asked no questions and bought it anyway. It wasn't long before he sold it, making a handsome profit. Well, the same fellow turned up a week later with an assortment of silver and gold things—of course it was Hasty—and in no time at all that river pirate had John where he wanted him. I think of him as a river pirate because he started out that way, but later he branched out and he and his men burglarized houses, stores, factories, you name it."

"But why did Pa—" I began.

"Look at it this way: Hasty needed a respectable businessman on whom to unload his loot, and John looked the part. Then once my brother accepted the very first piece of stolen goods, Hasty had him in his power. He could have exposed John at any time, ruined him.

Anyway, John went along with him, became wealthy, married Flora, had a child—well, you know the rest."

"Not quite," I said quickly. "Why were some of the stolen goods brought here on the boat?"

"Oh, that was one of John's ideas. Whenever he thought some articles might be recognized as stolen he sent them here—over my objections, mind you—and after he died Hasty wanted to keep on bringing them. They're all gone now; I took the last of them over to a dealer in Riverhead. Slim chance that anyone out here will recognize any of them."

"Simon, did Hasty kill Pa?"

"It certainly looks that way," he answered. "When I was in the office with John that morning he told me that Hasty had become greedy. He wanted seventy-five percent of the take instead of the twenty-five they'd agreed on years earlier, and John wouldn't give it to him."

"So the men who came to the house that night, or else Hasty himself, murdered Pa because he wouldn't meet Hasty's demands. Is that right, Simon?"

"Yes, I'm pretty sure it is," he said, rubbing his chin very much the way Pa used to when he had something on his mind. "I know it's unusual for blackmailers to murder their victims, but they've been known to do it—in a fit of rage at being frustrated. Also, Hasty knew that John kept a large amount of money in his safe at home, probably more money than Hasty'd ever had in his life. And the safe was empty when I got there. Did you see it?"

"Yes, I did. The books had been pulled out and thrown on the floor, and the door to the safe was open," I answered, remembering the horror of that morning.

"Well, I think that's what happened, Emily. John refused to give Hasty and his men what they demanded, and he had to pay for that refusal with his life. I was sleeping in one of the rooms above the office that night when Hasty came to tell me John was dead and, I suppose, to see what I intended to do. From that moment on I've wanted to bring Hasty to justice, but I needed time to come up with a way of doing it without becoming involved myself. And I had to see to your safety. I'd promised John I would. He thought if anything happened to him you might be in danger.

"Then Hasty managed to have me arrested—I've told you about that—and I landed in the Tombs. Fortunately I have a good lawyer who sorted things out. Your sketch of Hasty was a great help to the police. Thank God he's back in jail now. Before I left the city I heard he'd been charged with the murder of the night watchman of a warehouse, among other things."

"Will he be tried, Simon?"

"Yes, indeed, and he'll hang."

"Poor Pa," I sighed. "First Ellie's accident, then Flora's illness and death, and finally his own dreadful murder. He was such a kind man. . . ."

We sat quietly for a few minutes, and when I saw Simon turn his attention to some papers on his desk I stood up to leave.

"Simon," I said, pausing at the door, "I think I'd like to stay here for the rest of the summer, and then see—"

"Of course, of course," he said warmly, "as long as you like. And Emily, now that you know the whole terrible story, don't think too badly of John. He couldn't help himself. He was a man possessed by ambition and by love of a beautiful woman."

❧

As the August days slipped by, some of them hazy and hot, others crisp and cool, I was able to spend considerable time with my painting. I even sold a few landscapes to a shop over in New Suffolk.

"The summer people buy 'em, miss," the

proprietress said when I showed her a small painting of the dock where the wherry was tied up, "but the natives aren't interested. You should go to New York for the winter. Oh, this one sure is pretty!"

"Perhaps I will go to the city," I said, thinking of Herr Lubin and the classes I'd like to attend. Suddenly a picture of Hugh Carberry leaning against the door of the art studio flashed across my mind, and I realized I hadn't thought about him very much since . . . since when? Of course, it was when I was at Madame's house in Church Street, right after I'd seen the announcement of his engagement in the paper, and after that I'd cried myself to sleep several nights in a row. That was when I knew I could not afford to let my thoughts dwell on him.

⚱

"Is something wrong, Emily?" Simon asked, coming out to where I stood on the porch late that evening, wondering if Hugh would bring his bride to New York and if I would have to meet her. "You seem unusually quiet tonight."

"Oh, no, not really," I answered. "Just a slight headache. I think I'll go up to bed now. A good night's sleep should cure it."

"Poor darling," Simon said softly, putting his arm around my shoulders. "I hate to think of you not feeling your best."

I tried to disengage myself, but before I could he took a firmer hold on my arms and turned me so that I was facing him.

"Look at me, Emily," he said huskily, lifting my chin so that I had to look into his intense dark eyes. "You're incredibly lovely, you know—"

"Simon, I—"

"I know you are still young, young enough to be my daughter, but you are *not* my daughter, and I am a man with normal male desires. I love you, Emily. I want to marry you. I'll give you whatever your heart desires—I'll move to the city, anything. Oh, God! How I want you for mine!"

Before I could speak he crushed me to him with one arm, and still holding my face in his other hand, kissed me passionately on the mouth before releasing me.

"Simon, please listen—"

"No, no! Don't answer me now. I know this was sudden, too sudden, maybe, but now you know how much I love you, my darling. I've wanted you for years! Think, Emily, how happy we'll be!"

"For years, Simon? How can you say that?

You've only known me for six months or so."

"Figure of speech, my darling," he said quickly. "It seems as if I've known you forever, and I want you to live with me as my wife for what is left of forever. No, no—no more talk tonight. Go on up to bed and cure that headache. Here, let me kiss you good night, my love, my lovely one. Tomorrow we'll make plans."

ᴈ· *Chapter XX* ·ᴈ

I SLEPT HARDLY at all that night. Simon's declaration, coming as it did when my thoughts had been lingering on Hugh Carberry, not only shocked but also frightened me. He had seemed so sure of me, so convinced that I had no choice but to consent to marry him. But how could I? Aside from the fact that I found it difficult to believe he'd loved me ever since we first met, literally over Pa's dead body, the thought of any kind of intimate relations with him was repulsive, even nauseating.

I must leave and go to Madame as soon as I can, I thought. Maybe tomorrow. But the train fare, where will I get it? Sell the painting I did last week? The one with the view of the house from the road? But will Simon try to stop me? I'll have to lie, tell him I need some things in Mattituck and get Josh to row me across.

Eventually I fell asleep, but not for long. A

wind sprang up sometime during the night, causing the shutters and windows to rattle, and a little while later I heard rain pattering down on the roof of the porch, just outside my window. A comforting sound, that, I thought, and drifted off into an uneasy sleep.

❧

"Billy says it's a nor'easter coming, Em'ly," Paul greeted me when I appeared at the breakfast table the following morning. "Guess we'll be in the house all day. Wanna play checkers, Papa?"

"Maybe later, son," Simon answered. He had risen from the table to hold my chair for me, and after he pushed it in he let his hand rest on my shoulder.

"I'll show you some games, Paul," Tenth said, handing me the basket of hot muffins. "Rainy day games, my mama called them."

"Checkers?" he asked hopefully.

"Yes, and some others, too. But not until I get this kitchen cleaned up."

Ordinarily I would have reveled in the warmth and comfort of the big kitchen, the good smells of bacon and coffee, the blaze of sparks when Billy added another log to the fire, and Anna's cheerful face as she kept her eye on the plates that were passed to her for more of

240

the food she had cooked. But I was too ill at ease, too unnerved by Simon's watchfulness, to enjoy anything that morning. He rarely took his eyes from me, as if he were waiting for an answer, a nod or a smile that would indicate my acceptance of his proposal of the previous night. I found it difficult to concentrate under his scrutiny and had to make a definite effort to join in the conversation with the others. It wasn't easy, and by the time the meal was over my mind was racing, trying to figure out how I could slip away, get across to the mainland when the wind and the rain were so strong.

I'll have to wait until the storm is over, I thought, as I carried my dishes to the sink. Maybe I'll spend the day in my room. No, Simon might come in and ask me—oh, how am I to get through this day? Shall I just tell him, tell him that marriage is out of the question and that I'm leaving? That might be—

The sound of heavy footsteps in the center hall made me whirl around. A moment later the door to the kitchen was flung open, and the bright chatter around the table stopped as Jack Hasty entered the room.

Someone left the front door unlocked, I thought hysterically, standing perfectly still. Nobody moved or spoke. Hasty stood just inside the door, and the group at the table looked as if they'd fallen under a spell—it could have been the opening scene of a play, before the characters went into action. Then Simon stood up.

"Don't move, Simon," Hasty barked. "If ya know what's good for ya ye'll stay put."

"Look, Jack—" Simon began.

"Jack!" Hasty exclaimed with a snort. "That's what yer brother called me. You never said anythin' but Hasty, not that it made any difference to me."

"All right, Hasty then," Simon said impatiently. "Say what you want—"

"What do I want? An' how did I get here? Izzat what you wanta know?"

"Actually, no," Simon answered. "I want you to leave now, at once."

"Not so fast, mister. Thought I was back in jail, eh? Well, yer not the only one with friends in high places, lemme tell ya. An' I came here on the *Flora*. Nice little boat, that one."

"For God's sake!" Simon's temper was rising.

"No, fer my own sake," Hasty shouted. "That's why I come, an' I'll go all right. Who'd want to stay in this godforsaken hole? But I want the rest of the money you owe me, an' I'll take the girl, too, the one over there by the sink. An' the little boy."

"Emily!" Simon gasped, "and Paul—"

"Yes, Em'ly," sneered Hasty. "She wuz brought to me years ago—a little flower she wuz—an' I let Mag take 'er to Fat Sally. An' now she's in full bloom, and I want 'er back. An' I'll take the boy, too. Teach him how to make a livin'."

"Paul, no, no!" I cried. "I won't—"

"C'mere, girl!" Hasty ordered. "Yer goin' with me."

"No!" Simon shouted. "She stays here, and Paul—"

Paul huddled up against Anna's skirts as both men started for me. As Simon moved in front of him, Hasty whipped out a slungshot— a replica of the one John Ireland had carried— from one of the large pockets in his coat and swung it at Simon with all his strength.

Simon went down on the stone floor of the kitchen with a dull thud and lay still, the long fingers of his right hand stretched out as if he were trying to take hold of my skirt. Hasty wasn't satisfied. Within seconds he produced an evil-looking knife and brought it down on the back of Simon's leg. Almost immediately I heard a howl of pain from Hasty and looked up in time to see Billy pin the pirate's arms behind his back while a brown liquid dripped down his face. Tenth had hurled the still-hot contents of the old enamel coffeepot at him with deadly accuracy. Josh quickly produced a rope, and between them he and Billy secured Hasty's hands before marching him out into the rain and the howling wind.

❦

The slungshot had caught Simon across his thigh, and for the two days while we waited for the weather to clear so that we could send for the doctor he lay in extreme pain, either from that blow or from the knife gash in his leg. He was delirious at times. Billy carried him upstairs before he regained consciousness—the doctor said later that he'd hit his head hard when he fell on the stone floor—and we made him as comfortable as we could in his large four-poster bed. He opened his eyes several hours later and struggled to sit up, only to fall back on the pillows, groaning and calling for help.

From then on he lay still, with short intervals of sleep interrupted by half-lucid waking moments when he would call out for various people: Flora, Aunt Becky, myself, and others whose names I did not recognize. Whenever he said "Emily" I held his hand, hoping to quiet him, but I might as well have been holding fingers made of putty for all the good it did.

"He'll pull through, Miss Emily," Dr. Simpkins said when Josh was finally able to row him across the bay. "His thighbone is broken, and his knee's been injured as well, but I've set those bones. He'll be in considerable pain for a while, and the leg will never mend perfectly, but he'll be able to get around with crutches first, and then a cane. He's also had a concussion, and some fever, but I'm more worried about the gash on the underside of his leg than anything else. There's been some infection there; I've cleaned it out and told Billy how to change the dressings. Someone should be with him constantly so he doesn't do himself an injury. I've left some laudanum, in case the pain is too severe, but never give him more than two drops in water three times a day. Feed him anything he wants, and send Josh over for me in two days' time."

ༀ

The following week was a tiring, trying time for all of us. Simon was not a good patient. His mind cleared, but he complained constantly of the pain in his leg and was so irascible that Paul refused to go in to see him. Changing the dressing on the wound was the hardest chore. Simon swore, screamed, and struck out at anyone who touched it, even Dr. Simpkins.

By the end of ten days the doctor said he saw a gradual improvement, but that didn't make my life any easier. I remember sighing with relief one evening when Anna came upstairs and sent me down to the kitchen for a cup of cocoa.

"Then you go right to bed, miss," she said firmly. "Me and Tenth will be here, and then Josh will take over. He's sleepin' now, so's he can watch later."

Billy came into the kitchen while I was there, poured himself some cocoa, and sat down across from me.

"Good news, Miss Em'ly," he said, settling himself comfortably. "I'm willin' to bet we've seen the last of Jack Hasty."

"What makes you say that, Billy?" I asked, hoping he was right.

"Well, you see, when me and Josh took him outa here and down to the cove, I wanted to throw him in the water, but that fellow Doakes was there with the *Flora*. We had a bit of a scuffle, an' it ended up with Doakes takin' Hasty on board. Josh and I stayed until we caught our breath, an' then we took off. It was pourin' rain, remember, and the wind was a fair gale. So I don't know whether they sailed that day or not."

"He might have come back here," I gasped.

"Aw, no, miss. He was too beat up, an' he couldn't see good after Tenth threw the coffee at him. Anyway, I wasn't down there again until this afternoon, and do you know what I saw? Jack Hasty's top hat floatin' around in the water, and the big rock that was up on the cliff had fallen into the mouth of the cove. In the storm, I guess. Rain musta loosened it. There's no way now a boat can get into the cove; the channel's blocked."

"Do you think the *Flora* was wrecked? And that Hasty and Doakes were drowned?"

"Dunno, miss. Could be, but I didn't see any pieces of her floatin' around. Just the hat. That was some nor'easter, wasn't it? Remember the noise the wind made? There's trees down all over the road."

⚜

The next day, taking Shamrock with me for company, I went down to see the cove for myself. It was just as Billy had described: the top hat had washed up against the rocks near the shore, the huge rock that had been outlined so magnificently against the sky had indeed fallen from the promontory, and the opening from the cove into the Sound was so reduced in size that only a small canoe could have gained entrance.

I must paint this, I thought, as it is now, in contrast to the way it was. I must stay here long enough to do that. I walked slowly to the house with Shamrock gamboling along near me, covering at least five times the distance I did with her forays into the woods and futile chases after the alert birds of the island. Back in my room I studied my original picture of the cove for a few minutes, remembering how upset I'd been at Simon's reaction to it and understanding now why he hadn't wanted me to go near it. No, I don't think I'll paint it again, I thought. This is the way I'd like to remember it.

"He's all right, miss," Tenth said as I went into the sickroom a little later. "A bit fevered but quiet enough. Best keep a cool cloth on his head."

She smiled encouragingly at me and slipped away, closing the door quietly behind her.

When I changed the cloth on his forehead, Simon opened his eyes and reached for my hand.

"You're better today, aren't you?" I asked.

"Yes, oh, yes," he answered, speaking rapidly. "So much better, my love. You've no idea what the sight of you does for me. Ah, Emily, remember all the times you and I were together, how we were nearly always alone in the evenings?"

I assumed he was talking about the nights we'd sit by the kitchen fire after Paul and the others had gone to bed, but when he spoke again his words made no sense at all.

"You were—I had you to myself then. I didn't have to share you with anyone, not until Madame came to tell you it was bedtime. And remember our shopping trips and our dinners out? And the studio I arranged for you, where I could sit and feast my eyes on you while you worked? And the bracelet—and where is the little cat pin with the diamond eyes that I bought for you that day in A. T. Stewart's Emporium? Ah, Emily, my dearest, surely you belonged to me then. . . ."

I stared in horror as his eyes closed and the full import of what he'd said struck me. He wasn't Simon. He was Pa, impersonating his brother. Otherwise he couldn't possibly have known all those things. He'd planned it all! As Simon he could start wooing me afresh, denigrating his real self so that as Simon he would appear to an advantage. Even trying me out with that casual offer of marriage! And, as Simon, blaming all the trouble with Hasty on his old self. Ah, Hasty! Hasty almost caught him out when he called him Jack! It all fits, it all fits. Why didn't I suspect?

I sat beside the bed like someone in a trance while I went over past events. He'd said that night on the porch that he'd loved me for years, and maybe he had. He deliberately tried to keep me on Grape Island, appealing to my better nature when he asked me to take charge during his absence, and he'd known just what kind of paints and canvases I liked, he knew— he knew everything about me! And now I know everything about him, I thought, all except two important facts: Did he kill the real Simon? And why?

⁂

During the night it occurred to me that I might find the answer to that question, as well as to some others, in the office downstairs. Some paper or document might give me a clue. If anyone wondered about my presence in the office I could always say that Simon asked me to look for something for him. But then, no members of the household had ever shown any curiosity about Simon's private affairs, any more than they'd questioned the identity of the man who brought Anna and me to Grape Island. Pa, I reasoned, got away with his impersonation successfully not only because he was Simon's identical twin but also because he'd lived on the island for years, and even after he left it he'd been back to visit often enough to be able to stay abreast of what was going on.

Even so, I thought, it is remarkable how he fooled everyone, even little Paul. He must have put on the real Simon's clothes the night of the murder, the clothes Simon had left in the John Street house, so that he'd smell like his brother, and of course they would have fit him. Then I remembered the perfunctory, almost uncaring way he'd buried the real Simon—and Aunt Becky! He'd seemed relieved when she died, and with good cause, I thought, remembering how she whispered that she was "not sure about Simon" just before she died. Pa was fortunate, yes, but he was also careful, almost meticulous about details, and he almost got away with his grand plan.

⁂

As I sat down at the old, somewhat battered rolltop desk in the pleasant office, I remembered the long hours the purported Simon had spent there when I first arrived on the island. He'd probably been copying over, altering, or destroying whatever was in the real Simon's handwriting, I decided. Everything seemed to be in order when I went through the various drawers and boxes. There were copies of the bills of sale for the house on Colonnade Row and for the one on John Street, as well as recent notes from two different banks acknowledging fairly large deposits. I could find no reference whatsoever to antiques, jewelry, or other valuables. Pa must have destroyed any records Simon had kept of goods that ended up on Grape Island.

What care he gave to every single detail involved in establishing his false identity! If I hadn't been so appalled by the deception I think I would, at least at that moment, have admired his cleverness. After I found the letters, though, I felt nothing but resentment, scorn, even hatred for him. There were two of them, both addressed to me. They had been tossed carelessly in the back of the last drawer I opened. Perhaps he had heard someone coming and wanted to get them out of the way in a hurry.

Pa must have picked up the mail that day, I thought. Josh would have given them to me at once. Both letters had been opened and, I'm sure, read by him. When *I* finished reading them my relief—no, my joy—knew no bounds.

Spring Lake
July 25, 1859

Dear Emily,
Don't pay any attention to the news of

252

Hugh's engagement. He is home from England and is writing to you himself. I hope this letter reaches you before his. He had a dreadful experience while he was abroad. He will explain everything to you. I hope you will understand and consent to see him. He is perfectly wretched and worries because he hasn't heard from you.

Believe me, he never proposed to Lady Enid Grenville, never had any such intention. He had met her on three or four occasions and then was invited to a dinner party at her parents' house. She is older than he is, and he was not attracted to her, but to be polite he accompanied her into the conservatory after dinner was over. She insisted that he proposed to her over the roses and lilies! Of course he did no such thing, but her mother, who had stationed herself among the ferns, said she heard him ask her daughter to marry him and announced the engagement the next day.

Poor Hugh was at his wit's end. He finally went to Lord Grenville and told him the whole story, explaining that he had no interest at all in his daughter. Lord G. laughed and said this had happened once before and that he didn't know what he was going to do with his wife and child. Then *he* notified the papers that the announcement of the engagement had been a mistake.

Hugh heaved a sigh of relief and sailed for home as soon as he could. He's deeply in love with you, Emily. Be kind to him, please. We both miss you.

Sincerely,
Carrie

Spring Lake
July 25th

My dearest Emily,

I wouldn't blame you if you refused ever to see me again, but I hope with all my heart that you will permit me to come out to Grape Island and tell you in my own words what was involved in that ridiculous episode in England. In *one* word it was entrapment, or an attempt at entrapment.

I am on vacation from the firm at present, so would be free to travel to see you at any time you name. Believe me, my darling.

All my love,
Hugh

I had intended to write my letters of explanation to Hugh and Carrie at once, but no sooner had I taken their two envelopes up to my room for safekeeping than I heard shouts and then screams from the sickroom. I hurried across the hall to find Billy holding the invalid's shoulders down on the bed, trying to keep the pain-crazed man from throwing himself on the floor, while Anna attempted to stanch the flow of blood coming through the bandages on his leg. I sent Josh off for Dr. Simpkins at once and then measured out a dose of laudanum. Billy held the sick man's arms firmly while I raised his head and held the glass to his lips. A merciful silence descended on the room as the drug began to take effect, and just before his eyelids drooped, Simon (Pa?) looked up and said that he loved me.

⸸

Dr. Simpkins's face was grave when he came down to the parlor later that evening.

"I cleaned out the wound again, Miss Lawrence," he said in a tired voice, "but I don't like the look of it, I don't like it at all. I'm afraid it's gangrenous and that the leg will have to come off."

"How could that have happened?" I asked. "We were so careful."

"Nothing you did or didn't do, my dear," he said quickly. "You told me that he was first struck with a slungshot—filthy things they

255

are—and that broke his thighbone and injured his knee, but it didn't cause the blood poisoning. He was then cut with a knife, a knife that must have been far from clean, which cut deeply into the leg. And then, you see, the weather being what it was, it was almost three days before I got here, giving the wound ample time to become infected."

"What do we do now, Doctor?"

"We must convince him that the leg has to be amputated or else he'll die," he answered.

"He'll never consent, I'm afraid."

"Then we'll have to force him. I'll be back in the morning."

⁂

The next day Simon was too weak to protest about anything. When Dr. Simpkins came with a stretcher and extra men to help transport him to the hospital in Riverhead, he took one look at his patient, came back downstairs, and told his helpers to wait at the dock for him.

"I'd stay if I could, Miss Lawrence," he said, taking both my hands in his, "but I have a number of sick people to see, and besides there's nothing anyone can do now. It's all over, you see. I've given him something for the pain. Let me know when he goes. It won't be long."

After that there was nothing to do but wait, turn the pillows, smooth the bedclothes, and watch for signs of suffering. The end came early one evening when the sun was low and the birds were beginning to chirp what Paul called their "good-night songs" to each other. I was alone with the dying man at the time, and in view of what he said then I am glad no one else was there. I had just lighted the oil lamp and moved it to the little table next to my chair when he opened his eyes, smiled, and whispered my name.

Almost without thinking I said softly, "Pa, did you kill Simon?"

Without a moment's hesitation he answered, "But of course. There was nothing else to do. Simon was becoming a damn nuisance, demanding more and more. I never liked him, and he never liked me. We fought like animals when we were boys. Jack Hasty had threatened to kill me, and I knew he meant it, so when Simon came that night I had a brainstorm: we looked so much alike that no one, not even Aunt Becky, could tell us apart, and I knew Hasty would be fooled. So when Simon went for the safe I was ready, and in a matter of minutes he was strangled. And Hasty never knew who it was—"

He coughed then, and after brushing aside

the water I offered him he smiled and spoke again. "And so, in a way, I killed myself, fooled everyone."

He coughed again, and I heard what I knew must be the death rattle in his throat before he lay still, his dark eyes staring sightlessly at me.

ʾ

We buried him in the old cemetery in the clearing in the woods, not far from where his brother and aunt lay, and when Josh made a sturdy wooden marker with *Simon Lawrence* painted on it I said nothing. I saw no point in letting Paul know that the man he thought was his father had been his father's murderer.

We had a subdued lunch after the brief ceremony, and later, instead of going upstairs to rest as Anna suggested, I walked slowly down toward the dock to try to clear away thoughts of the past and turn my mind to Hugh and the future. First, I thought, as I came to the water's edge, I must get in touch with Simon's—or Pa's—lawyer.

At that moment I was distracted by the sight of a small boat approaching our dock and completely unnerved when the man at the oars turned and looked directly at me. Even without his top hat there was no mistaking Jack Hasty, and for a moment a wave of utter terror enveloped me.

I turned and fled back the way I had come. Simon was dead, the boys would be in the barn—how could I stop Hasty from entering the house and seizing Paul, who would be taking his afternoon nap? I was running as fast as I could when my eye lighted on the end of one of the island's ropelike grapevines protruding onto the path. I picked it up, and holding it firmly in my hand, dragged it along the ground and into the bushes on the opposite side.

Moments later Hasty came pounding along, and when I judged him to be almost even with me I raised the vine to knee level, hoping he wouldn't see it. He didn't. I watched him fall headlong and lie still. Several minutes elapsed before I had sufficient control of myself to be able to creep out of the bushes and make my way back to the house.

❧

"Yep, he's dead, Miss Lawrence," Dr. Simpkins said when he came into the kitchen with Billy and Josh later that afternoon. "Gave his head a good whack on that piece of ledge rock. Those city shoes he was wearing weren't meant for running in the woods. Must've slipped on the wet weed growing there. Accidental death. I see a lot of them in these parts, most of them drownings, though."

"He shoulda had his top hat on," Billy said grimly. "Woulda broken his fall."

"Might've," the doctor said, "but I doubt it. Well, I'll send the sheriff's men over, and they'll ship him back to the police in New York, this time in a wooden box."

I suppose grapevines were too prevalent on the island for the one on the path to cause comment. In any case, no one mentioned it. I kept my own counsel, and that night before I slept I tried to justify my action. I had never intended to *kill* Jack Hasty. I had only wanted to prevent him from taking Paul and forcing me to be his "woman." No one ever knew what really happened, and I can say in all honesty that my conscience has never troubled me.

⋅ *Chapter XXI* ⋅

"SOMEBODY'S COMIN', EM'LY," Paul said, pointing out across the bay. He'd been rather quiet and withdrawn since Simon's death the previous week, and I was glad when he begged me to take him down to the dock so that he could try out the fishing pole Josh had made for him. The idea of treading on the spot where Hasty had fallen did not appeal to me, but when we came to it I saw that the rain of the night before had left it looking just like any other part of the path, and I knew there was nothing to be afraid of on the island anymore.

"Somebody's comin' here, Em'ly," Paul said again. "Look, he's wavin' at us! Who is it?"

I shaded my eyes, and as the boat came closer my heart began to beat faster and the whole world seemed brighter. Moments later Hugh was folding me in his arms, kissing me and murmuring endearments. He kept it up until the fisherman who had ferried him across coughed and asked if the gentleman would be returning. In the meantime, Paul, impatient to get on with his fishing, had settled himself on the side of the dock and dropped his line in the water.

இ

"I came as soon as I received your letter, Emily," Hugh said when we were sitting on the sunny dock in a pair of old canvas chairs we found in the shed. "In fact, if your letter hadn't arrived yesterday I intended to come anyway. Carrie told me you had probably seen the announcement that crazy Englishwoman put in the paper, and then when you didn't answer my letters I was afraid you'd either rejected me or that something had happened to you."

He took both my hands in his, then, and leaning forward, put his face close to mine. "You don't reject me, do you, my darling? Say you believe me when I say I love you more than life itself!"

"Oh, Hugh, I do love you. I've loved you since—"

"Stand up, Emily! I want to hold you in my arms. No, don't say anything. Just let me hold you."

262

Hugh stayed on Grape Island until the end of his vacation, a total of four days, during which time he heard not only everything that had happened to me since he last saw me but also the details of the Hasty episodes. He probably heard these last several times, since Billy and Josh were prone to dwell on them. He was absolutely horrified by my account of my trip on the *Flora* even though I tried to make light of it, and every time Josh or Billy mentioned Hasty's threat to take Paul and me away with him he looked so pained and troubled that I would try to change the subject. He was equally shocked when I related the story of Pa's deception and would say from time to time, "To think you were living with a murderer! The man was a beast!"

After a while I was able to get him to talk about his work, what he had accomplished in England, and what he thought the future held for him. He was enthusiastic about the law, liked the people with whom he worked, and was looking forward to rising in the profession to the point where he could open his own law offices.

The day before he left I took him down to see the cove, and when I pointed out the remains of the waterlogged top hat he hugged me to him and said he didn't think he could ever bring himself to wear one. Then with a last look at the strange, frightening beauty of the small enclosure, we turned away, leaving the quiet waters to a pair of gray and white seagulls.

※

"You'll be leavin' us, won't you, miss?" Anna asked after Hugh had gone. "An' I don't blame you one little bit. I remember lookin' out the upstairs window and seein' him bringin' you home to the city house, an' how he looked at you. I could tell—"

"I could take you with me, Anna," I said. "After all, I brought you here."

"No, miss, but thank you. I think I'd better stay here, for a while, anyway. Josh and Billy and Paul need someone."

"Maybe you could take me, miss," Tenth said quietly. "I could work for you and Mr. Carberry, and I'd like to see what the city is like. I didn't have much of a look at it before, and besides, I still don't see any way of getting to Canada."

※

Things worked out pretty much as Anna and

Tenth had wanted them to. Hugh and I were married early in October and moved into a house on Charles Street, one that he had picked out because it had an artist's studio with a good north light on the third floor. It was also convenient to his office, and with the help of some of the members of his firm he was able to settle the muddled estates of John and Simon Lawrence without undue delay.

Paul, as Simon's son, inherited Grape Island and would come into possession of the brothers' accumulated wealth at the age of twenty-one. In the meantime the trustees would provide the funds necessary for the maintenance of the house on the island as well as for Paul's education and living expenses.

Hugh and I wanted the little boy to live with us in the city for the school year and spend his summers on the island, but during a trial visit to Charles Street Paul was so homesick and miserable that we had to take him back to Anna and Josh and Billy. We thought we'd try it again when he was older, but he never wanted to come. He grew up out there very much the way his father had, except that he had Anna instead of Aunt Becky to boss him around. Anna, who married Josh the following summer and produced three sturdy boys in rapid succession, treated Paul like one of her own. She stood for no nonsense from anyone in what, over the years, she came to consider her household, and they all adored her.

Tenth did come to work for us, and unlike Paul, she loves city life. She intends to stay, she tells me, but adds that maybe when she's an old lady she'll go back to take a look at Virginia. Billy still has not left the island, even though Miss Acker has long since gone to her reward. He says he's too old and set in his ways to make any changes now. He surprised us the last time Hugh and I went out to see how they were all getting along by saying he had something he wanted to show us.

"It's out in the barn, Miss Em'ly," he said. "I've kept it in a safe place. I thought you and Mr. Hugh would like to see it."

I don't know what I expected to see as I watched him reach up to a shelf above one of the windows and take down something wrapped in a piece of burlap, but it certainly wasn't a piece of wood about fifteen inches long with the letters FLOR faintly visible on it.

"Found it down at the cove after the last storm we had," Billy said proudly. "Must have been there some time by the look of it, maybe caught under one of the rocks. Means the *Flora* was wrecked, don't it?"

"Indeed it does," I answered. "And it explains why Jack Hasty had to come over in a rowboat. What about the top hat? Is that still there?"

"No sign of it, Miss Em'ly," he said, shaking his head. "It's gone, like Hasty himself, an' no loss to anyone, if you was to ask me."

ঌঌ

Later on that day Hugh and I stood on the grassy knoll, the very spot where I had set up my easel years before, and looked down at the treacherous calm of the water below us.

"It's beautiful, Hugh," I said with a slight shiver. "More than beautiful, it's magnificent, but I can't help feeling that it's haunted—and I'm not ordinarily a superstitious person."

Hugh chuckled and put his arm around me. "Whatever evil may have lurked here in the past has been laid to rest, my darling, even if Jack Hasty's uneasy spirit has been condemned to inhabit these watery depths for all eternity— looking for his top hat, maybe?"

ঌঌ

When we returned to the city I removed my painting of the cove from the wall in the drawing room and put it in the back of a closet in my third-floor studio, where it is to this day. Perhaps sometime I'll be able to look at it with pleasure, but for the present it is better hidden, like the cove itself.

Center Point Publishing
Brooks Road ● PO Box 1
Thorndike ME 04986-0001 USA

(207) 568-3717

US & Canada:
1 800 929-9108